# TORN
# ALLEGIANCE

## THE WANDERER SERIES
## BOOK THREE

D1316894

# G. MICHAEL HOPF

## DEDICATION

TO THE FAMILY AND FRIENDS WHO HAVE
SUPPORTED ME NO MATTER WHAT.

"The friend in my adversity I shall always cherish most. I can better trust those who helped to relieve the gloom of my dark hours than those who are so ready to enjoy with me the sunshine of my prosperity.

- Ulysses S. Grant

# PROLOGUE

"I have always found that mercy bears richer fruits than strict justice." – Abraham Lincoln

## TWENTY-TWO MILES SOUTH OF ST. JOSEPH, MISSOURI

## NOVEMBER 17, 1876

The loud bang of the heavy door slamming shut woke John. He opened his eyes to find he was immersed in darkness. He struggled to move but quickly discovered his arms and legs were bound. *Where am I?* he asked himself. The last thing he recalled, he had been asleep when men came into his hotel room and knocked him out.

Wanting to sit up, he struggled but eventually got into a sitting position.

"Who is that?" a voice called out from the darkness.

"Garrett?" John asked, recognizing the voice.

"John, is that you?" Garrett called out from across the pitch-black room.

"I think we were double-crossed," John said.

"It appears that way," Garrett said with a sigh.

"Any idea where we are?" John asked.

Garrett looked around but, like John, saw nothing. "Wherever they have us, it's the darkest place this side of hell. Last thing I remember is looking up and seeing two men; then everything went black. Now I'm here."

"My entire body hurts, and my head is throbbing. I guess they must have done a number on me. Say, are you tied up too?"

"Yeah, like a hog," Garrett quipped.

Faint chatter hit their ears.

"Who is that?" John asked.

"Ssh," Garrett said, hoping to hear who it could be and what they were saying.

The voices grew louder until they almost sounded as if they were in the room. The sound of keys followed by the clack of a heavy dead bolt told them, whoever it was, they were coming inside.

The door creaked open. A faint glow washed over John and Garrett. Standing in the open doorway were two shadowy figures. One quickly entered the room, grabbed Garrett by the arm, and pulled him to his feet. In a raspy voice the man said to his compatriot, "Get the other one."

"My feet," Garrett said.

The man pulled a knife and cut the bindings around Garrett's ankles.

The second shadowy figure came in, marched over to John, and stood above him. "Get up."

"If you'll give me a minute, I'll do just that," John said, straining to rise.

Impatient, the man took John by the arm and forcibly brought him to his aching feet.

"I can't walk," John said.

Like the other man, he bent down and cut John's bindings. "There, now move," he said and shoved John forward.

"Where are we going?" John asked.

"Just keep your mouth shut," the man barked.

John exited the room. The dim light took a second to adjust to, but when he did, he saw he was inside a barn. All around him stakes of tobacco hung drying, and the rich but pungent smell of the leaves overwhelmed his senses. At the far end John spotted Garrett sitting in a chair. Next to him stood a man, and next to him another chair sat, no doubt one he'd be sitting in.

The man pushed John along until he was in front of the chair. "Sit down."

John turned and plopped down in the chair.

The two men stepped aside.

John took a moment to look around and get his bearings. He didn't recognize the barn and had no idea where he was. Several oil lanterns lit the space, casting their orange light across the barn. He tried to spot anyone else but couldn't.

A door opened behind them.

Curiosity begged John to turn around and see who was coming, but fear of getting struck curtailed the desire.

Two men appeared to the side of John. They whispered something unintelligible then separated, with one taking a chair and placing it feet from John and Garrett. He was middle-aged and had a thick beard and deep-set eyes. His physical stature was average, and his attire told them he was a man of some means.

The second newcomer stepped past the seated man and leaned against a support beam. He pulled out a cigar, struck a match, and lit his cigar, puffing several times until the end glowed bright orange and thick puffs of smoke billowed all around him. He blew out the match, tossed it on the dirt floor, and stomped it with his boot.

"Who are you?" Garrett asked the seated man.

The man leaned back and replied, "Funny, I'm here to ask you the same question."

"I think you know who I am, so why not tell me who you are," Garrett said defiantly.

The man chuckled and said, "You're right. I know who you both are and what you are. I just wanted to see what you'd say."

Garrett leaned forward and squinted. His eyes widened when it dawned on him who it was he was talking to. "Wait a minute, you're Frank James."

The man turned around and looked at the smoking man behind him.

The smoking man nodded as he took a long inhale of his cigar.

Facing Garrett once more, the man said, "You're right. I am Frank James, and the man behind me is my brother Jesse. We heard you were sent to find us. Well, you have, but I can tell you this one simple fact. Soon, you'll regret you ever did."

"Are you planning on killing us?" Garrett asked.

Jesse stepped from the shadows and walked up next to Frank. He removed the cigar from his lips, looked at Garrett carefully, and answered, "One of you will die for sure; the other, well, you're going to help us with some critical information."

"What sort of information?" Garrett sneered.

"There's a train coming in from Denver, arriving in a couple of days. Word is it's loaded with something valuable."

"We don't know what you're talking about," Garrett said.

John watched the exchange and had a distinct feeling that if Garrett didn't shut up, he'd end up with a bullet in his head. Hoping he could negotiate, John said, "How about you let us *both* go?"

"Now, you see, that's not going to happen. We need to send a message to your boss back in Chicago, and the best way to do that is by sending him parts of one of his men," Jesse said.

"What sort of information are you looking for?" John asked.

Garrett shot John a look and barked, "You don't negotiate with people like this."

"I'm trying to keep both of us alive," John said.

"By striking a deal with criminals?" Garrett asked.

"I believe these men can be bargained with. Hell, everyone has a price," John said.

Jesse stepped forward and said, "There is no deal. We're already aware of the train; we just need to know what's on it."

"I won't tell you anything," Garrett said defiantly.

"If you keep us both alive, I'll tell you what's on the train, and I'll sweeten the pot with some information you'll definitely need," John said.

"Don't you dare make a deal with them." Garrett

seethed with anger at John.

John ignored Garrett and asked, "Do we have a deal?"

Frank and Jesse looked at each other.

Jesse stepped forward and asked, "Not sure, what's on the train?"

"A carload full of United States Treasury notes."

"What in the hell would we do with new notes? They'll be able to track them," Jesse said.

"No, these are all previously issued notes. They're coming from the treasury in Denver and headed to Washington, DC. It's to do with the Resumption Act; they're to be destroyed," John explained then added his sweetener. "But I can understand your concern, so I can connect you with a man in Texas who can help you rid yourself of them in exchange for gold coin."

"What does he do with the notes?" Jesse asked, curious.

"Does it matter?" John asked.

"Humor me," Jesse said.

"He takes them to Mexico and other parts south and exchanges them for foreign currency. It's some sort of exchange-rate scam. I met the man who runs this racket a couple of years ago. He helped me track down someone. He's a good man to know," John confessed.

"Interesting," Jesse said then tapped Frank on the shoulder and signaled for them to step away.

Frank got up, and the two walked to the far corner of the barn.

"What the hell are you doing?" Garrett asked.

"Stalling for time. Now play along," John replied.

Garrett cut him a look and whispered back, "You don't play games with these people."

"We either play games, or one of us is dead tonight. I'm going for games until we can figure out how to get out of here, and not in a box headed to Chicago," John said under his breath.

Jesse and Frank returned.

"You have a deal, but we're not letting either one of you go until we know what you're telling us is true," Frank said.

"Damn it, John, you can't make deals with people like them," Garrett lashed out, but this time he was going along with the ruse.

"I just did," John countered.

"These men are liars, thieves and murderers," Garrett roared.

John locked eyes with Jesse and asked, "We can trust you, right? If we give you the details of the train and where to move the notes, you'll let us go?"

"As a gentleman of Missouri, my word is my bond," Jesse replied. "As far as a matter of trust, it's you two traitors that I have a hard time trusting. How can sons of the South turn their backs on their own people and side with the Yankee occupiers?"

"The war is long over. Time to move on," Garrett replied, this time not acting.

Jesse strutted over, yanked the cigar from his mouth, and blew smoke in Garrett's face. He gritted his teeth and seethed, "The war never ended. We're just fighting it differently is all."

Garrett shook his head.

"Take this one away. Lock him back up," Jesse ordered, pointing at Garrett.

The other two men in the room grabbed Garrett and hauled him back to the room.

Jesse took a seat on the now vacant chair and said to John, "You're going to tell me everything you know about this train, and you best not be lying."

"I'm not lying," John confessed.

"There's an entire train car full of notes?" Jesse asked.

"That's what I've been told. To be clear, I don't have all the specifics, but what I don't know, I can find out from the Chicago office," John said.

"What do you think, Frank?" Jesse asked his brother.

"It could be true, but he could also be stalling. Have we ensured we got them all?" Frank asked, referencing if any other Pinkerton detectives were in the area.

"It's just me and him, no one else that I'm aware of," John said.

"I heard it's just these two," Jesse answered Frank. He turned to the other men, who had just returned from locking Garrett back up, and ordered, "Cut him loose." He adjusted his stance and placed his hand on the back strap of his Colt.

One of the men stepped forward and cut the rope bindings holding John's arms together behind his back.

John rubbed his sore wrists, gave Jesse a look and asked, "How did you know me and my partner were

Pinkertons?"

Jesse smiled and said, "Telling you isn't part of our deal."

John stood waiting for what would happen next.

"You're John Nichols, correct?" Jesse asked.

"Yes, and how do you know my...real name?"

"I won't tell you, I'll show you instead," Jesse said, motioning for John to follow him.

John did just that and exited the barn just behind Jesse. The cool air of the early evening felt good, as did the fresh air.

Jesse stopped midway to the house, took John by the arm firmly, and said, "We have ways of finding out information. We have people, loyal people, everywhere, or people ready to take a payout; so don't think you're going to lie to me without me eventually finding out."

"Mr. James, my will to live far outweighs my need to protect that train full of notes; and I'll be honest, while the war was many years ago, I still haven't forgotten what the Yankee invaders did to my wife and child."

"They killed your wife and child?" Jesse asked, genuinely curious.

"Yes, sir, they were murdered by a detachment of bummers," John replied.

"My condolences for your loss," Jesse said sincerely.

"Thank you."

"A Southern gentleman like yourself, who fought for the Confederacy and even had his wife and child murdered, turns his back on his own country, then ends up working for the very people who murdered his family.

Makes no sense, nope, doesn't at all. I don't understand how some people think," Jesse said, shaking his head.

"A man needs to eat," John said.

Jesse patted his shoulder and said, "What good is nourishing your body if your soul is starved of righteousness? Now let's get inside. There's someone I want you to see."

# CHAPTER ONE

"I have heard something said about allegiance to the South. I know no South, no North, no East, no West, to which I owe any allegiance." – Henry Clay

## MILLS FARM, SOUTH OF ST. JOSEPH, MISSOURI

## NOVEMBER 5, 1876 (TWELVE DAYS BEFORE)

Helen Mills stood on the edge of her biggest field, clasped her hands together, pressed her eyes closed, and prayed that come spring the fields would be full of workers planting next year's crop of tobacco. This was an exercise she did nightly, though her prayer would vary depending on the time of year.

The years since the war ended had been tough on her. Having lost her husband fighting alongside William Quantrill and his Raiders, she was left with over two hundred acres of fertile land but no real experience in tobacco farming. The foreman who had worked on their farm also died in the war, and the slaves who once worked the fields had all left. She was a widow, with a vast expanse of land and no knowledge on how to tend to it. However, Helen Mills wasn't about to give up. It wasn't in her spirit to do such a thing. This land had been in her husband's family for generations, and letting it go wasn't an option. By the summer of 1867, she had planted a successful crop, and each year following she did the same. Her success grew, and soon she had acquired more land and expanded the business. Many in town praised her, but she gave all thanks to God, for she felt this was his blessing upon her for all the suffering and sacrifice she had endured.

The sound of a horse riding hard broke her thoughts and tore her away from her prayers. She turned and saw someone in the distance riding hard towards her house. She had an idea who it was and grunted at the unexpected visit. Since early summer Graham Hooper, a widower and tobacco farmer who owned an adjacent farm, had been trying to court her.

She had no desire for him, and it wasn't due to his appearance because he was a handsome man by local standards. It wasn't due to him being poor; on the contrary, he had more land than her, and his operation was profitable. Her main objection to his romantic overtures were due to his behavior during the war.

Though he was old enough to fight for the Cause, he'd chosen to stay; but it wasn't out of cowardice. He chose not to fight because he was an anti-secessionist. Although his political beliefs weren't born from pride or an unwavering patriotism for the Union; no, it was solely pragmatism. He couldn't see how the South would ever be victorious due to the North's clear manufacturing advantage. He was a betting man and put all his chips, so to speak, on an eventual Union victory. His gamble paid off, and when the war ended, he found himself rich with land and the owner of the only tobacco distribution warehouses in town.

Helen could never marry him. Her love for the Cause ran deep, so deep that it was her prodding that had seen her husband join to fight with Quantrill. Losing him, then the war, was almost unbearable, she would not then completely surrender by marrying a man whose allegiances ran counter to hers. Never.

Graham slowed the horse to a trot and jumped clear of it. "I won. I won!" he shouted excitedly.

Always making sure to remain pleasant around him, she asked, "Won what?" though she knew what he was referring to.

"Mrs. Mills, you're now looking at the new sheriff of Buchanan County," Graham said, taking a slight bow for theatrics.

"Congratulations…Sheriff," she replied.

"Oh, Helen, this is so exciting, and might I add that it could be good news for us too," he said, once more making a subtle overture of marriage, something he did every time he saw her. He was a relentless man and wouldn't quit until he got what he wanted. He removed a handkerchief from his pocket and wiped his brow. "May I get my horse some water?"

"Of course," she replied out of courtesy.

He took his horse by the reins and walked it to her stables. Upon his return, he said, "It's a bit warm, isn't it, for early November?"

"I find it quite cool myself," she said, tugging at the shawl that draped her shoulders.

He wiped his upper lip and said, "Say, could I get a

glass of water?"

Unable to refuse, she answered, "Yes, of course. Where are my manners? Please come inside."

He followed her inside the house and stopped just inside the foyer. "Is Abigail here?" he asked, referring to Helen's house servant. Abigail had been Helen's house slave until her emancipation and subsequent freedom were granted after the war. With nowhere to go, Abigail had stayed and was now employed by Helen.

"She's not. I sent her to town to get some provisions, but Gabriel is; he's in the barn," Helen answered, swiftly walking to the kitchen to pour him a glass of water. Gabriel was Helen's twelve-year-old nephew. He had come to live with her as an infant during the war because both of his parents had died, his father in the war and his mother shortly after. The stress of losing her husband was too much, so she took her own life. Helen had welcomed him into her home with open arms and showered him with as much love as she could, treating him like her own child. He was a good boy and worked hard around the farm. Gabriel didn't go to school due to having Down syndrome. Helen had him go the first year, but the local children were relentless and abusive, so she felt it best to school him at home.

Graham followed her into the kitchen and looked around. "You keep a tidy home, Helen, and it always smells so sweet."

Feeling his presence weighing on her, she poured the water and handed him the glass.

He took it and noticed her hands were shaking ever

so slightly. "Oh dear, you're shaking. Are you okay?" He put the glass down on the nearby table and took her hand in his.

She recoiled from his touch and said, "You should drink your water; you look flush."

"My dear Helen, you're the one who looks flush," he flirted.

She turned away from him and said, "I'm feeling tired. I couldn't sleep last night."

"I'm sorry to hear that. How about we sit in the parlor? I want to tell you my plans as sheriff and how it can benefit both of us. Also, I'm being sworn in late tomorrow, and you'd honor me if you were in attendance."

"Now, Graham, we've had this conversation before. I don't wish to have it again," she said, her body tensing knowing he was about to get aggressive with his fawning.

He brushed off her comment and continued, "Apparently, they found votes in the bottom of a sack at the second precinct. I won by thirteen. Can you believe it, thirteen votes? That's my new lucky number going forward." A large grin graced his smooth face. "I'd like it if you wore that blue dress I've seen you wear at church."

"Graham, I won't be wearing the blue dress—" Helen said.

"Why not?" Graham asked, interrupting her.

"Because I'm not going to your ceremony. It's not appropriate. I don't want people to get the wrong idea about us," she answered bluntly.

"Now, Helen, you'd be my special guest. You'd make

me very happy if you came," Graham pressed.

"I can't. I have important things I'm doing tomorrow as well. I'm acquiring some additional land, and I need to get the surveyor out to verify the boundaries."

"Why?" Graham asked, his face showing a mix of anger and disappointment.

"Because I need to know the exact boundaries, that's why," she replied.

"Not that, why won't you come to my swearing-in ceremony?" he pouted.

"I'm not doing this anymore with you. We're never going to be what you want," she snapped.

He raced around and confronted her. "Helen, my dear, you're a widow, I'm a widower. I own a tobacco farm, you own one. My farm sits on your boundary; we're neighbors. We share so many things in common except the same name and the bed. Be my wife. I swear to God I'll love and cherish you. You're young enough to have children still, and with both of us childless, that alone would be the blessing of our union together."

She stared at him coldly and said, "No."

"Why? Tell me one good reason why?" he asked, his tone shifting slightly, showing his annoyance.

"I've told you before. I don't wish to remarry. When I die, I wish God to join me with my one true love in heaven."

"Helen, that is foolish and naïve talk. You're too young to stay unmarried. You have many years ahead of you. You can't wish to remain like this until you're old," he said.

"I do."

"Do you know what people say about you in town?" he asked.

"I don't care what people say."

"They say—"

"I said I don't care. Now please go," she said, stepping away from him and motioning towards the doorway.

"I won't leave until you give me the answer I came for," he said, grabbing her arms aggressively.

Startled, she said, "Let go of me and leave while you still have your dignity."

"Why do you treat me this way? I'm a good man, I've worked hard, and I've built a successful business and thrived. I can be a good husband," he pleaded.

Unable to hold back her real thoughts, she blurted them out. "Hard work? You stole people's land. You stayed while others fought for our country. You preyed upon those poor widows who lost their husbands and hand no way of keeping their land. No, Graham, you're not a good man."

His eyes widened with shock. "This is about the war? After all these years you still hold hatred because I didn't run off like the other fools to die for a cause that was hopeless."

"Let go of me and leave...now," she snapped.

He ignored her and squeezed her arms tighter. "I won't leave until you give me something. I've waited patiently for years for you to come around. Never have you said you harbored these feelings."

"You're hurting me!" she howled.

"I will not leave."

She struggled to free herself but couldn't. Welling up with anger, she lashed out, "You're a gutless coward and predator. I would never marry you. In fact, every time I see you, my skin crawls. You might think my husband a fool, but he was a hero, a brave man who fought for something he believed in, unlike you. You stayed and lay with all those snakes in the grass. You're pathetic!"

His anger swelled until it burst. "You may feel this way about me, but one thing I am that you can't take away is that I'm the sheriff and have more power than I've ever had, and what happens here will be your word against mine." He threw her against the table.

Her face smacked against the top of it, and her chest hit the edge, knocking the wind out of her.

He lifted her dress and ripped at her undergarments.

"No!" she wailed.

The front door opened with a loud creak. "Mrs. Mills, I'm home," Abigail hollered, wiping her shoes on the foyer rug.

Hearing Abigail, Graham stopped his assault. He straightened out his clothes and leaned down until his face was next to hers. "If you say anything about this…I'll…"

She replied by spitting in his face.

He wiped the spit off and rushed off. He passed Abigail in the front room and didn't say a word.

"Good day, Mr. Hooper," Abigail said.

He raced out the front door, slamming it behind

him.

"Mrs. Mills, you here?" Abigail called out, sensing something was out of sorts.

Helen appeared in the front room. "Hi, Abigail, please take the items to the kitchen."

Seeing her face was red and that she had been crying, Abigail asked, "Mrs. Mills, you okay? Did that man hurt you?"

"Abigail, please take the items to the kitchen," Helen ordered and walked to the large bay window that overlooked the front of the house. She pushed aside the drapes and saw Graham riding away in the distance. Under her breath, she said, "If it's the last thing I do, I'll kill you, I swear it to God."

## ASKEW FARM, SOUTH OF ST. JOSEPH, MISSOURI

John had only been in Missouri for a couple of days, but his body was feeling the long days of physical work.

Daniel had him working from dawn until dusk. There was a lot to be done on a farm this size, and when you were the only laborer, it meant going from one task to the next with hardly a break in between.

Although his body ached, he enjoyed the work. It brought back memories of working his fields back in Georgia. He could never understand how any man could work at a desk. He had been a hands-on person from his youth and took great pride in ending a day with dirt on his hands and sweat on his brow. He also enjoyed seeing the fruits of his labor; if he had wood to chop, he took pride in seeing the split wood stacked and that job done. Nothing like a day of small accomplishments.

He had rushed to get his work done because today he was set to meet up with Garrett in town and exchange any intelligence each might have gathered on the James brothers.

Garrett was working in town as a porter in one of the tobacco warehouses. Garrett wasn't like John; he didn't enjoy the work and more so hated the fact he spent many days inside a darkened warehouse.

John washed his hands and raced inside the house to quickly change his clothes. Inside, he found Daniel standing over a bucket in the kitchen, peeling potatoes. Daniel was a widower, having lost his wife a couple of years back to influenza, and after losing his son at the hands of the James and Younger gang, he would hire people like John to help him around the farm year-round.

John felt sorry for the old man and swore to himself he'd do his best to make good on helping him while also doing his primary job of hunting down the James brothers. "I'm gonna head into town. I got the barn cleaned and the stakes all stacked and ready for spring."

"Before ya do that, I need ya to run by the Mills farm and pick up somethin' for me," Daniel said, his head bent over the potatoes.

"Where's the Mills farm?" John asked.

"Take a right at the end of the drive; go a quarter mile to the large oak that has three notches. Just after that, take a right and head up her drive," Daniel explained.

"Okay. What am I picking up?" John asked.

"Just some paperwork is all. Now hurry on, I'll have dinner on the table at five thirty," Daniel said.

"I'm going to change then head out," John said, heading towards the stairs.

Daniel turned around and gave John a peculiar look. "Gettin' pretty, are ya?"

From the top of the stairs, John hollered back down, "Not getting pretty, just don't want to smell like one of your hogs."

## KANSAS CITY, MISSOURI

Frank Bradley wasn't accustomed to receiving letters, so when the postman stopped at his apartment, he first thought it might be someone coming to collect a bounty on him. The irony in his thinking was because he was one of the most notorious bounty hunters and outlaws in the Midwest. A former Union Cavalry officer who had served under George Custard during the Civil War, he was a man familiar with fighting and tracking down his enemy from horseback. His exploits following the war had won him fame in the newspapers and in some penny novels, but it also made him a pariah in the law's eyes and a target himself.

"Just shove the letter under the door and go away," Bradley said, his voice raspy and thick.

"Yes, sir," the elderly postman said, bending down and pushing the small letter under the door. "Good day."

Bradley curiously looked down at the letter, almost

afraid to pick it up. When he saw the return address was MINNESOTA TERRITORIAL PRISON, STILLWATER, MINNESOTA, he snatched it off the floor and tore it open. He unfolded the single page and began to read.

*Dear brother,*

*As you know, I'm five years now languishing in prison for a crime I didn't commit. I have petitioned the governor, but to no avail, as the words I write must fall on deaf or uncaring ears. I have never written you mainly because I feel shame, not because I have done anything wrong except loiter with the wrong people. You warned me before my unfortunate situation to separate myself from those associations, but I didn't listen to the wisdom from my older brother. Oh, how I wish I had.*

*I am not writing to complain, nor am I writing to seek forgiveness for my foolish ways. I feel if you were to give it to me, you would without me asking. I am writing because I know the line of work you are in and I have information that could enrich you.*

*I am sharing a cell with Mr. Cole Younger, THE Cole Younger from the James-Younger Gang. He is a nice gentleman, gracious and talkative. He has shared with me something that you will find valuable. One night while we both lay awake talking, he shared with me the story of his first robbery. He detailed how he and his infamous partners, Jesse and Frank James, along with others robbed a Union gold shipment headed to Louisville, Kentucky, from Nashville, Tennessee. I don't send this thinking the gold is somewhere to be found. I send this because two of the people involved in the robbery are living close to you in Missouri, in a town called St. Joseph. They might know the whereabouts of the James brothers, as I heard they are hiding out, possibly in St. Joseph. I can only imagine the bounty for them is high, and if you could find them, not only would you benefit financially, but the glory and fame could be profitable as well. The names of the people in question are Michael McKinney and Helen Mills.*

*I pray this information helps, and if you could ever see it in your heart, a letter from you would always be welcome. Be well, my brother.*

*Your little brother,*

*Charles*

Bradley folded the letter and placed it on the small table near the front door. He dashed to his bedroom and began to pack a small bag. He didn't need any convincing, he would be on the next train to St. Joseph, and hopefully soon, he'd be capturing two of the most famous outlaws in history.

## MILLS FARM, ST. JOSEPH, MISSOURI

John followed Daniel's directions perfectly. In no time he had ridden to the front of the house. He dismounted his horse and tied it to a post near the front steps. The house was two stories, with a wraparound covered porch and wood siding. The white paint on the siding was peeling, and from the overall look of the house, it needed some maintenance. He scaled the steps, but before he could reach the front screen door, it opened, and there before him was Gabriel.

"Hello, mister, what do you want?" Gabriel asked.

"Hello, fine sir, is your father here?" John asked, not knowing anything about the familial situation. Daniel had neglected to tell him anything about the Millses.

"No, sir, my daddy died in the war…and my mommy killed herself, tied a rope around her neck and—"

"Gabriel, go tend to the chickens," Helen blurted out, emerging from the house behind Gabriel.

"But I already tended to the chickens this morning," Gabriel said.

"Then go tend again," Helen said and rushed him off.

Gabriel turned and left.

"Hi, I'm so sorry about Gabriel. He likes to overshare, as they say," Helen said, wiping her hands on her apron.

"That's quite alright," John said, quickly noticing Helen's natural beauty. He immediately forgot himself and stared at her.

"What can I help you with?" Helen asked, giving John a once-over.

John cleared his thoughts, removed his wide-brimmed hat, and said, "I'm so sorry, excuse me for my rudeness. My name is John Nance. I'm the new laborer who works for Mr. Askew. He sent me over here to get some paperwork."

"Yes, the paperwork for Daniel," Helen said and turned around. "Please come in and have a seat in the parlor. I'll be right with you."

John came into the house and entered the parlor. Instead of sitting, he looked around at the porcelain trinkets and tin photographs that adorned one of the bookcases near the front door.

Helen came back into the room and held out a scroll of papers fastened together with thick lace. "Tell him I agree to the terms. I'll have the notary come if it all looks good. Just remind him I need to know a good date to order it."

John took the scroll and smiled. "Nice set of figurines," he said, motioning to the bookcase. John wasn't the least bit curious as to the transaction between Helen and Daniel.

"You appreciate those silly things?" she asked, shocked that a man would give two seconds' thought to such items.

"I wouldn't say I appreciate them; they're more of a sentimental reminder. My wife used to have a couple, and my daughter loved to stare at them. It took every ounce of self-control for her not to play with them," John said with a slight smile breaking across his stubble-covered face.

Helen stepped towards the bookcase and gently took one into her small hands. "My husband would give them to me on my birthday. I think he liked them more than I did," she said with a bittersweet tone.

"Your husband was killed in the war?" John asked.

Helen put the figurine back down and turned to face John. "Yes, he was," she said sadly.

"My condolences."

"Thank you," she said, folding her hands in front of her. "I'm thinking of selling some of these. Would you have interest in them for your wife?"

"Oh no, um, my wife, she passed away years ago," John replied.

"Then maybe your daughter?"

"She passed too," John said.

"Oh dear, forgive me. I'm sorry," Helen said, her face flushed. A moment passed before a smile graced her face. "Look at us, both without spouses, talking about childish porcelain trinkets."

John was having the hardest time not staring at her. Outside of her silky auburn hair and gentle, almost angelic features, her radiant blue eyes kept pulling him in each time he looked into them. She had a magnetism that he hadn't felt in many years. It was an allure that far outweighed the feelings he'd had for Katherine back in Tucson. What could it be? He'd only met her minutes before, but there was something about her he was drawn to. Needing to leave before he made a fool of himself, he said, "I'd best be going, thank you." With the papers in his hand, he turned and went towards the door.

"Tell Mr. Askew I look forward to hearing back from him soon," Helen said, walking past John and opening the door for him.

John exited and turned to face her. "It was nice to meet you…" he said, leaving a pregnant pause with hopes she'd give him her name.

Picking up on his cue, she said, "Now look who's

being rude. My name is Helen Mills, and it was a pleasure to meet you as well."

John put his hat on and nodded. "Good day." He stepped off the porch, grabbed his horse and mounted it. Just before riding off, he glanced to the front door to see if she was still there...she was. Once more he nodded then rode off.

## ST. JOSEPH, MISSOURI

"You're leaving already?" John asked, shocked as he watched Garrett pack his bag.

"Yes, based on what you told me and on credible information I've gathered, it's best I head south to Nashville while you stay here," Garrett said, stuffing his bag with his clothes.

"Shouldn't we stay together?" John asked.

"No, we need to move on credible information as soon as we can. Mr. Pinkerton wants us to find the James brothers as quickly as we can."

"If you're so sure they're in Nashville, why don't I go too?" John asked.

Garrett looked up from what he was doing and answered, "Because we don't know for sure. All we have is information that must be verified."

"Why not contact Chicago and have them send a team to Nashville?" John asked.

"I've been working for Pinkerton for four years; this is my break. If I find the James brothers, I'm sure to get a promotion. I'm not about to let someone else get the credit; I'm going to be the one," Garrett said, fastening his bags and grabbing his gun belt. "No contacting Chicago at all unless it's an emergency; they must not know."

"That seems wrong. This could all go sideways," John said.

"We'll be fine. Let's go down as the team that caught the James brothers," Garrett said, his mind flashing images of him being paraded around and celebrated for the achievement.

"What do I do? How do I contact you?" John asked.

"John, you'll be fine. You've survived much more than this. Keep your ear to the ground; track every lead you get. If they're here, then you'll reach out to me and wait until I return. Don't do anything without me," Garrett said. "Promise me."

John didn't reply.

Garrett looked at him squarely and said, "Promise."

"I promise," John said. "How will we communicate?"

"Every few days I'll send a cable. We'll keep it encrypted. If nothing has changed, I'll simply say the weather is cloudy. If I say clear skies, then you'll know I've located them and to come immediately. Use the same phrase when messaging me too," Garrett answered.

"Got it—cloudy don't come, clear skies come," John said, nodding.

Garrett patted John on the shoulder and said, "We're close. I can feel it."

"I hope so," John said.

"Be careful and watch your back, okay?" Garrett said, slinging his bag over his shoulder.

"I will; you too," John said, the shock not wearing off. The last thing he'd expected when he saw Garrett was to have him promptly leave.

"I'm serious, watch your back. The locals love the James brothers. Be very careful how you gather intelligence; you don't know who you're talking to all the time. The Jameses have little birdies everywhere singing for them," Garrett warned.

"I'll be careful, I promise, and please let me know as soon as you can if you find them," John said.

"I've got to go. The train leaves in less than an hour," Garrett said and raced out of the boardinghouse room.

John stood and waited. The last thing he wanted was both of them connected to each other.

After a few minutes, John exited and stepped out onto the street. Even though he hadn't seen Garrett every day, it was nice knowing he was close by. Now he was truly on his own again. It wasn't an unfamiliar feeling, and being the hunter was something he had a talent for after having spent eleven years tracking down each man responsible for the murder of his wife and daughter. He brushed aside any anxiety he felt and put himself into the same mindset he'd had before. He was there to do one job and one job only, track down the James brothers and bring them to justice.

# CHAPTER TWO

"Buy land, they're not making it anymore." – Mark Twain

## ASKEW FARM, ST. JOSEPH, MISSOURI

## NOVEMBER 6, 1876

John shoveled the eggs and bacon into his mouth, dripping yolk onto his chin. He wiped it with the available napkin before Daniel could complain about him eating like a hog, but Daniel didn't say a word.

Daniel was less talkative than normal. He sat and pushed his food around on his plate.

Noticing Daniel's unease, John asked, "Are you okay? I'm not used to sitting and eating in silence."

"It's nothin'," Daniel grumbled.

"After that response, now I know something is wrong," John said, concerned. "Maybe I can help."

"Do you have eight hundred and seventeen dollars to spare?" Daniel quipped.

John stopped chewing. He could see the weariness in Daniel's eyes. "What's happened?"

"Taxes, Goddamn property taxes," Daniel growled, tossing the fork onto his plate of uneaten eggs and bacon.

"You owe eight hundred and seventeen dollars?" John asked.

"I owe more, but after I sell that hundred acres in

the south, I'll be in a better position," Daniel explained.

"You're selling some land?" John asked, then suddenly realized that must be the transaction he was having with Helen Mills.

"Yes, Mrs. Mills is buying it. I'd sell her more, but she can't afford it," Daniel answered, confirming the transaction.

John began to think about the money he had, which totaled in the thousands, and whether he could help but stopped short of doing so when he could hear Garrett's voice in his head telling him to remain focused.

"By the way, after lunch, I need you to go take the signed documents back to Mrs. Mills. Tell her to order the notary for tomorrow, late, say three o'clock," Daniel said, getting up from the table, his plate of uneaten food in his grasp. He slowly walked to the deep basin sink and placed it there. As if that short distance was fatiguing, he leaned his entire weight against the sink and sighed.

John could see the visible stress in his frail body. Once more he thought of offering to help, but just as he was opening his mouth, he stopped himself. "I'll head over to the Mills farm when I'm done in the north field."

"Fine," Daniel said without looking at John, his head hanging low.

John finished his breakfast, placed his dish in the sink, and headed out to begin his day.

## ST. JOSEPH, MISSOURI

Graham paced his office, mumbling as he went back and

forth. He couldn't shake the encounter with Helen yesterday. Never a man to accept no for an answer, he wasn't about to give up, but what hurt him most was her painful comments. What disturbed him the most was that he wondered if others felt the same way about him. He thought not, since he'd won the election, although by a slim margin; he still had support in the community.

"I know people like me. I'm set to be sworn in soon as sheriff," he mumbled.

The election for sheriff was a special one, meaning he wouldn't have to wait until January to take the position. His swearing-in ceremony was set to take place later that afternoon. Having Helen there was something he had hoped for, but she had squashed that plan and simultaneously made him feel inadequate.

"How can I win her over?" he asked himself out loud.

Byron James, a county commissioner and longtime friend of Graham's, entered his office without Graham knowing. Overhearing his question, he asked, "Are you still trying to wed the widow Mills?"

Graham jumped; Byron's question startled him. He swiftly turned and asked, "What are you doing here unannounced?"

Byron put his bowler hat on a side table next to his walking stick. "I'm here on account that we had a meeting set this morning to go over tax delinquencies."

Graham's eyes widened when he realized he'd forgotten about the scheduled meeting. "Oh, yeah, I forgot; but is this appropriate? I'm not technically the sheriff just yet."

Byron removed a pocket watch, popped open the cover, and looked at the dial. "You're the sheriff-elect, and in six hours you'll be the sheriff of Buchanan County. The timing is just fine. Plus, we need you to get moving on asset forfeiture as soon as possible."

"Fine, come sit down," Graham said, taking a seat behind his desk.

Byron closed his watch, slid it back into his front vest pocket, and took a seat in the armed chair in front of Graham's desk. "I can only imagine that thirteen is now officially your lucky number."

Graham chuckled and replied, "It is, yes, it is."

"Say, before we get into all this paperwork, answer my question," Byron said, shifting in his seat.

"About Helen Mills?"

"Please tell me you're not still trying to court her. She'll never marry a Jayhawker like yourself; that woman probably wears her dead husband's Bushwhacker battle shirt under her dress. You need to let her go and go find a good Unionist woman. Once you're sheriff, you'll be a very desirable bachelor," Byron said.

Graham chewed on his lip. He hated that he'd been turned down by Helen, but what he hated most was that many in town knew about it.

"Please tell me you're not in love with her," Byron said, shocked at Graham's reaction.

"I do love her—there, I said it. I've had her in my sights since before the war. The first time I saw her, she was seventeen and had just married that son of a bitch husband of hers. He came down to a warehouse in town; he was selling a crop. Like a good wife, she waited for him. No doubt they were going shopping in town after he was done with his business. Her thick hair was pulled back, and she wore this pale blue dress, it was tight around her waist and her bosom was...it was so full. Ever since that day, I declared I would have her, and damn it, I will," Graham declared.

"You're serious; I had no idea. That explains why you turned down Maggie Smith's advances," Byron said, referencing a prominent widow in town.

"Of course you've known I've had my eye on Helen," Graham snapped.

"I thought it merely desire; I didn't know it was an obsession," Byron said with a slight chuckle.

"You think this is funny?" Graham growled.

"Of course I don't think it's funny. Forgive me, my old friend. So tell me, why won't she marry you?" Byron asked, leaning back and crossing his legs. If he was going to hear a long story, he was going to be comfortable.

Graham didn't reply right away; instead he looked past Byron and out through the window.

"It's fine, you don't have to tell me," Byron said, reaching for the folders that were sitting on the desk.

"You were right. It's because I sided with the Union," Graham complained.

"And you did so, like me, because you are a smart man. We both knew there was no way they'd win. Listen, my old friend, please forget about her. In fact, come with me at the end of the week. The widow Smith will be at the Harrisons' house for a party."

"No," Graham said.

"Oh, come on. It'll be fun, and you have an excuse to celebrate. You'll be the toast of the party, I guarantee it," Byron said.

"I have no interest in widow Smith," Graham snapped. He clenched his fists and gritted his teeth. "Let's get to work. I don't wish to discuss this further."

"Very well," Byron said, opening the first folder.

The two began to go over a list when the name Daniel Askew came up.

"Wait. Daniel Askew is behind on his property taxes?" Graham asked.

"Yes, by years. He successfully applied for the postwar exemptions, and as you know, they were due September 30. In fact, most of the people on this list were part of that program. And I don't have to remind you, this entire tax situation is the reason the last sheriff resigned. No one wants to be the collector; it doesn't get you invited to parties," Byron joked.

The postwar tax exemptions deferred property tax payments. Following the war, many had lost their livelihoods, and during Reconstruction, the county commissioners had passed the tax deferment exemptions. With Reconstruction long past and with the local economy rebounded, the county had voted to end the exemption earlier in the year and gave those who owed six months to pay. In Buchanan County, the sheriff was the government official responsible for collecting taxes. It was an unpopular and untenable situation for the sheriff, especially because many who had filed exemptions wouldn't be able to pay them back.

"Helen mentioned she's acquiring some additional land from someone. Do you happen to know who that is?" Graham asked.

A devilish smile broke out across Byron's face. "As a matter of fact, I do."

"Would it happen to be Daniel Askew?" Graham asked as his mind spun about how he could leverage this.

"Yes, it is," Byron said. "Why? What do you have in mind?"

"Does Helen owe back taxes?" Graham asked.

"From all the documents that survived the fire, the answer is no," Byron answered. The fire he referenced had broken out in the county clerk's office a year before and destroyed many files, including property tax liens, bills and payments.

"Did the Millses ever take advantage of the exemption?"

"I'm not sure. I don't have anything here showing that. She essentially has a clean slate, but many people took advantage of the law," Byron said.

"Who was the county clerk in the late 1860s?" Graham asked, his tone sounding urgent.

"Let me think. I believe it was Samuel Chase; he retired a few years back. He moved to Kansas City," Byron replied.

"Can we continue going over these records at another time?" Graham said, getting up and grabbing his wool jacket.

"Of course," Byron said. "Where are you going?"

"To send a telegram to Mr. Chase in Kansas City," Graham said, heading towards the door.

"But the swearing-in ceremony?" Byron said.

"I'll be back in time. I wouldn't miss that for the world," Graham said, slamming the door behind him.

## MILLS FARM, ST. JOSEPH, MISSOURI

John was looking forward to seeing Helen again, so much so that he got himself properly cleaned up this time. It had been a long time since a woman had affected him as much as Helen and as quickly. Yes, his time in Tucson with Katherine came to mind, but she was young, a child in many ways; Helen was different. She was closer to his age and responsible, not a youthful idealist needing to go conquer the world. Just from their brief encounter he knew they had much in common; how much he didn't know, but he wanted to find out. In the back of his mind he knew allowing himself to find interest in a woman wasn't professional given his mission was to track down the James brothers; but he told himself that a woman like her could know people, and from there he could find what he was looking for.

He rode to her house as fast as he could. The unusually warm November weather felt good against his skin as he pushed the horse to its limits. He made the turn onto her drive and only pulled back on the reins once he was mere feet from her porch.

As before, Gabriel appeared and greeted him, but

this time he was walking up with a basket in his hands. "Hi, mister, you here again?"

John dismounted, tied the horse to a post, and replied, "Hi, Gabriel; how's your day?"

"Good. One of the chickens was killed last night. A coyote must have gotten it," Gabriel said.

"Did it get into the henhouse?" John asked.

Gabriel held his head down and mumbled, "No."

"Then how did it get the chicken?" John asked, walking up to Gabriel. He peeked into the basket and saw a few eggs.

"I don't want to talk about it," Gabriel said, his head still hanging low. "I'm gonna go now." Gabriel rushed off towards the house.

"Ah, where's Mrs. Mills?"

A robust black woman walked onto the porch from the house, leaving the door open for Gabriel. Her name was Abigail, and she was Helen's maid and Gabriel's nanny. "You'll find the mistress at the henhouse," Abigail said, pointing to a couple of outbuildings that sat adjacent to the main house.

John tipped his hat and said, "Thank you." He pulled the scroll of papers from his saddlebag and headed towards the henhouse. As he approached, he took a deep breath and repeated in his mind several conversation starters. A slight breeze swept over him, bringing with it the familiar smells of a farm, from the earthy aroma of the dead leaves to the stink of the hogs and chickens. He'd only been in Missouri for a short time but found it like home.

Loud banging came from the henhouse. "Darn coyotes!" Helen groaned as she raked the feather-covered ground just outside the henhouse.

John stepped up and peeked through the fencing. "He'll be back, you know," John said, referencing the coyote.

Startled, Helen turned around quickly, placed her hand on her chest, and gasped, "Oh, you gave me a start. I didn't hear you coming."

"My sincerest apologies; not my intention," John replied, a look of concern on his face.

Helen put the rake down and stepped towards the gate. "I suppose you're returning the papers?"

"Correct, and Mr. Askew asks that you schedule the notary for tomorrow, around three o'clock," John advised.

Helen exited the chicken enclosure and walked up to John. She removed a handkerchief from a pocket on her skirt and wiped her brow. "Whew, I worked up a sweat."

"Yes, you did, but you still look nice," John blurted out and instantly wished he hadn't.

Helen blushed and asked, "Care for some tea?"

"I really should be letting you get back to work," John said, pointing at the henhouse.

"That can wait," she replied and stepped off towards the house.

John wasn't about to argue, so he followed. "Can I ask a personal question?"

"Depends on how personal," she quipped.

"You appear to be doing well. The farm looks good,

kept up, you're buying a hundred acres from Daniel, yet you're out here doing a laborer's job. Why don't you have workers?"

"I do, but they do things primarily concerning the tobacco business. As it pertains to my personal life, I like to do things myself. I have the money to hire, but after the long years during the war and the financial hardships I and others encountered, I decided not to take it for granted when times are good. It's best to save because the good times can easily become bad times," she answered with a striking confidence.

Her wisdom and strength astonished him. He smiled and said, "Makes sense to me."

They walked into the house to find Abigail and Gabriel in the kitchen, making a pie. When Gabriel wasn't helping out around the farm, he liked to assist Abigail indoors doing odd chores or cooking.

"Are you making apple pie?" John asked, his mouth watering at the thought.

"Yes, sir, I…sorry, we are," Abigail replied, taking a pinch of flour and tossing it at Gabriel.

Gabriel chuckled and continued peeling apples.

"Go relax in the parlor. I'll be right in," Helen said, going to the basin in the kitchen. She poured water over her hands and scrubbed them with a thick bar of soap.

John nodded and left the room. Back in the parlor, he continued where he'd left off yesterday and continued to sweep the room, looking at anything that could give him greater insight into who Helen was. He often found the things, no matter how small, that surrounded a person said a lot about who they were.

In the center of the far wall, a fire crackled in the brick fireplace. Above the mantel hung something very familiar to him, an 1861 Enfield Musket. He leaned in and looked more closely. The musket was clean and oiled, but it had seen battle without doubt. Its dark brown stock was covered in scratches with a few deep gouges. Much of the bluing on the barrel and other metal parts had rubbed off, exposing the steel beneath.

"It was my husband's," Helen said, walking into the parlor holding a tray. She placed it on the center table and asked, "Milk and sugar?"

"Ah, yes, please, thank you," John said, going to the chair next to where she was sitting, and took a seat. "Is that the musket he fought with?"

"It is. A dear friend of his brought it back and gave it to me. She was with him when he died," she said pouring the hot tea carefully into an ornate porcelain cup.

"Looks like it still fires," John said.

"It does. I've used it to kill a couple of deer," she said proudly as she handed him a steaming cup.

He took the cup and held it gingerly in his hand. "You hunt?"

"I wouldn't call it hunting. This time of year, deer will venture close. If it's a buck and I have a good shot, I'll take it."

"Impressive," he said, taking a sip.

"You learn a lot when times are tough. During the war, I barely managed to keep the farm going. I couldn't grow tobacco, but I grew some other crops and sold them at a market in town and gave much to our beleaguered troops."

"I have to tip my hat to you. I'm sure there were many predators circling, ready and willing to take your land away from you," John said.

"Those predators are still around," she said, bringing her cup to her lips and sipping.

"The world is full of evil, but it's also full of good God-fearing people who know right from wrong. Who stand up against those who would hurt the innocent," John declared.

"Are you one of those men?" she asked.

"Meaning?" John asked, ensuring he understood the question.

"Are you a man who stands up against evil?"

"I'd like to think so," he replied.

"Tell me, Mr. Nance—"

"Please call me John," he said, interrupting her.

"Very well. John, did you fight in the war?" she asked.

"I did."

"I believe I could presume for whom."

"If you're presuming based upon my Georgia accent that I fought for the Confederacy, you'd be correct," John answered with pride in his voice. "I was with the Sixty-First Georgia Infantry Regiment. I joined her ranks in '61 and fought all the way until '65. Sadly I witnessed General Lee surrender at Appomattox."

"God bless you for fighting. I only wish we'd defeated those blue-bellied bastards," Helen growled.

Her change in tone threw him off. There was no doubt in his mind now that she held a grudge against the Union.

"May I ask a personal question?" she asked.

"Sure," he said.

"Your wife and child. How did they die?"

He was prepared for any number of questions, but that one was very direct and personal. He froze, unable to find the right words to reply. Questions popped into his head about how much detail he should provide concerning their deaths. He normally didn't respond this way when it came to discussing his family, but for some reason a wave of emotions were crashing over him.

Seeing him unable to promptly reply, she said, "I truly apologize for my insensitive question. Here we were having a nice tea, and I'm asking barbaric questions. Please accept my apology."

"No, it's fine. It took me many years to move on from their untimely deaths. Only recently have I come to grips with it," he said softly, pausing again to find the right words.

"John, please forgive me. Losing loved ones is never easy. I still think of my husband often. To be honest, I think of all those beloved family members we all lost because of that wretched war thrust upon us."

John looked up at the ticking clock on the mantel and said, "I should be getting back. Daniel will complain otherwise."

Upset that her question was driving him away, she reached out and touched his hand. "Please forgive me.

We were having a pleasant time, and I had to ask a heartless question."

"Helen, it's fine, believe me. I have enjoyed my time with you, but I should be getting back," John said, placing his cup down and getting to his feet.

She stood and said, "I hope to see you again soon. Maybe after we formally wrap up this land deal, I can have you and Mr. Askew over for dinner."

"That would be nice," John said. "Have a wonderful day."

Helen escorted him out and watched as he rode off.

"Is it me, or do you have a twinkle in your eye for that man?" Abigail said, walking up behind Helen.

She turned, her face flush, and replied, "Have you been eavesdropping again?"

"Ma'am, it's my business to know everything that goes on around here," Abigail replied with a broad smile.

"I do like him. He seems like a good man. I noticed a sadness in his eyes yesterday, and now I know why, it has to do with his family. I fear something awful happened to them," she said, looking back and spotting John riding away at a full gallop.

"Sadness? Sounds like you two have a lot in common, ma'am," Abigail jested.

"Now mind your tongue," Helen quipped. "I feel I may have upset him though. I was prying too much."

"Don't you worry, ma'am, if he's a strong and good man, he'll be alright."

"I hope so," Helen said.

As Abigail headed back towards the kitchen, she said,

"It'll be nice to have a man around here. Lord knows Gabriel could use the influence."

Helen heard what she said and couldn't agree more. She'd been a widow for over eleven years. Having a man in her life she could trust and feel connected to was welcome. If that was John, only time would tell.

\*\*\*

John cursed under his breath as he rode back. He regretted his reaction to her simple but honest question the second he left. He'd never been so sensitive and could only think it was due to how open emotionally he had become in regard to her. Somehow in the short time they'd known each other, he was feeling something that was more than mere attraction, but how could that be?

Disappointed in his behavior, he swore to act differently the next time he saw her and promised that he would ensure that encounter would happen soon.

In the back of his mind, he could hear Garrett yelling at him to stay focused, but again he convinced himself that being close to her wasn't exactly not doing his job. Today's encounter had indicated that she held contempt towards the Union because of her husband's death; this could mean she could be a sympathizer and possible supporter of the James brothers. She was a major landowner in the area and a successful businesswoman; therefore her influence and reach were greater than most. It was probable that she knew a great many people and could possibly confirm if the James brothers were there or not.

Either way, it made sense for him to remain in contact with her, but there was a case for him to be made that getting closer, even intimately closer, could put him in the position to find critical information. With those counter thoughts, he dismissed Garrett's pesky voice in his head.

With a determined goal of courting her to find information, he needed to present himself in a better light, but just how was another question he didn't have the answer to just yet.

# CHAPTER THREE

"In this world nothing can be said to be certain, except death and taxes." – Benjamin Franklin

## ASKEW FARM, ST. JOSEPH, MISSOURI

## NOVEMBER 7, 1876

Loud banging at the front door tore John and Daniel away from the breakfast table.

"Who the hell is that?" Daniel roared with irritation.

John didn't like unknown visitors. While Daniel sauntered to the front door, John raced up the stairs, bounding two to three steps at a time until he reached the second floor. He sprinted into his bedroom, grabbed his Colt, which he had hidden under his pillow, and cocked the hammer. His ears perked up as he listened to who it might be.

More banging on the door.

Daniel unlocked the latch and swung the door wide. "Who the hell is hammering at the door?"

"Good morning, Mr. Askew. Sorry for the early morning visit, but I'm Sheriff Hooper," Graham said, standing on the other side of the screen door, his right hand resting on the back strap of his Colt pistol and his left hand tightly gripping a stack of papers.

What life Daniel had in his face quickly drained, as he knew exactly why Graham was there. "For Christ's sake, can't you give me a bit more time?"

"So you know why I'm here?" Graham asked.

Hearing it was the sheriff, John uncocked the pistol carefully and slid it back under the pillow. He stepped out of his room and stood at the top of the stairs, where he could hear better.

"Well, you ain't out here to sell me muffins. I know what I owe, Sheriff. I'm working right now to get that paid; I just need more time," Daniel said, his tone signaling that he was annoyed.

"Mr. Askew, the county gave you a tax-deferred status for over eleven years. As you're aware, tax deferred means you still owe it, just later—"

"I know what the damn word means," Daniel growled.

"Mr. Askew, you don't have to be rude," Graham said.

"So what are you here to do?" Daniel asked.

Fed up with Daniel's disrespect, Graham unfolded a paper and held it up for Daniel to see. "Mr. Askew, Buchanan County has placed a lien on your land and all the improvements because of your severe tax delinquency—"

"Get the hell off my property!" Daniel yelled at Graham. He opened the screen door, forcing Graham to step to the side for fear of being hit by it. Daniel snatched the paper from Graham's hands and tore it up. "Get off my land! I'll be damned if I let a Jayhawker sheriff come and take my land! This has been in my family for generations. It's never gonna happen, you hear. Get off my land!"

John rushed downstairs and stepped outside. His main concern was Daniel doing something that would only make things worse, not that yelling at the sheriff was helpful.

Upon seeing John, Graham stepped back and tightly wrapped his fingers over the grip of his pistol. "You two stay back," Graham warned.

"No one is going to attack you, Sheriff; that I can assure you of," John said slowly. "Daniel, come back inside."

"Not until this yellow-bellied Jayhawker gets off my land!" Daniel roared in anger.

"Who are you?" Graham asked.

"I'm John Nance, a laborer," John answered.

"So you have money to pay laborers but not to pay your taxes," Graham questioned with a snarl. His heart was racing fast with anticipation the situation could turn violent.

"Leave!" Daniel said.

"Daniel, you're not helping. The sheriff is only doing is job, nothing more," John said.

Daniel scrunched his face and gave John a mean look. "You sidin' with this scoundrel?"

"I'm siding with prudence and objectivity," John said.

"Listen to your laborer," Graham said. "You have the option of paying off the lien before then, but if not, I'll hold an auction next week."

"Sheriff, can't you convince the powers that be to

give him some more time?" John asked.

"I don't know who you are, but I suggest you start looking for a new employer," Graham said as he stepped off the porch, his gaze firmly planted on Daniel.

"Go, get, you coward!" Daniel yelled.

"Daniel, stop. You're not helping your predicament at all," John warned, taking Daniel's arm.

Daniel shrugged off John's grip and snapped, "Don't touch me."

"Mr. Askew, if you can't pay the lien by next week, make sure you have your personal effects and belongings packed. What's not carted off before the sale conveys with it to the new owners," Graham said.

Daniel pushed John out of the way and walked into the house. He reappeared with a double-barreled side-by-side shotgun. "I said go!" he screamed at Graham.

Graham raised his left hand, and fear gripped him as he stared down the twelve-gauge barrels. "Daniel, you're making a mistake. Threatening a sheriff is a crime in and of itself."

"And so is killin' one. If you're gonna arrest me for threatenin' ya, I might as well kill ya," Daniel said and raised the shotgun to his shoulder.

John stepped in front of Daniel and said, "Put the shotgun down."

Seeing an opportunity to leave, Graham climbed on his horse and rode off. Just before he was out of earshot, he hollered, "I'll be back next week and with my deputies."

Daniel lowered the shotgun and gritted his stained

teeth. "I should toss you out for sidin' with that son of a bitch."

"I wasn't siding with him, Daniel. If you shot him, they'd hang you," John said.

"It's a better death than lettin' them bastard politicians take my land. While many of us have suffered, those slick-talkin' sons of the devil have gotten rich off us. They're only going after us for back taxes 'cause they want our land, nothin' more. It's a damn scheme, I'm tellin' ya, a scheme."

"I'm sure it is, but let me help you," John said.

"And how is a poor laborer gonna help me? You don't have that kind of money. Hell, son, you ain't got two pennies to your name," Daniel said.

John paused before answering right away as he contemplated how he'd explain to Daniel that he had enough money to help him out. "What if I could get the money?"

Daniel raised an eyebrow and asked, "I'm not getting' involved in anything illegal, nope, you hear me? I don't want any part of that." He walked back inside the house.

John followed him and said, "Daniel, wait up. I have a friend, a wealthy friend. I can get the money." Once more John was lying. His life since he had gone looking for Captain Pruitt had been one lie after another. He'd promised himself he'd get back to being honest, but here he was pretending to be someone he wasn't.

"And what kinda interest or collateral is your friend gonna need, huh? And the terms? I go from saving it from the county to losing it to your friend. I'd rather die than lose this farm," Daniel said and disappeared into the house.

John didn't pursue him or press the issue. He felt he'd already said enough and was on the edge of compromising his undercover work. He had to stay focused on the mission he had been sent there for. He went back onto the porch and sat down on the weathered front step, his weight making it creak. Like before, he heard Garrett's voice booming in his head to *keep it together*. Speaking of Garrett, a telegram was supposed to come from him today.

The door burst open, and out came a flustered and irritated Daniel wearing his jacket and hat. He passed John without acknowledging him and headed towards the barn.

Concerned, John leapt to his feet and called out, "Where you off to?"

"That ain't none of your business. I'm not paying ya to mind me but my farm. Now best be gettin' to your work," Daniel growled.

John stopped and watched as the old man shuffled off. Moments later he emerged from the barn atop his favorite horse, Alice. "Yah, yah!" Daniel hollered.

Alice reared and sprinted down the drive.

John shook his head. He didn't know where Daniel was going, but wherever it was, the old man looked determined.

## MILLS FARM, ST. JOSEPH, MISSOURI

Gabriel twisted the barbed wire as hard as his small hands would let him, his face grimacing with each turn. His tongue jutted out from his mouth, something that was typical of him when he was focused on a singular task.

"That's it. One more turn then cut," Helen said, observing Gabriel's work proudly.

Making the final twist, Gabriel set the pliers down and picked up a pair of snips and cut the barbed wire.

"Excellent job," Helen said.

"I did it," Gabriel said enthusiastically.

"That's one, thirty-some more to go," Helen said, her hands planted on her hips.

Taking a firm grip of the wire, Gabriel shook it and said, "That will keep those coyotes out."

"That's what we hope," Helen said.

The sound of galloping pulled her attention away from the henhouse fencing and towards her drive. There she saw Daniel riding hard.

"You keep working. I'll be right back," Helen said to Gabriel, who merely nodded and promptly went to the next post and began working.

Daniel pulled the reins hard, causing Alice to rear back. Displaying an agility not common for a man his age, he climbed off and walked towards the front of Helen's house.

"Daniel, over here!" Helen called out.

He stopped his march when he heard her cry, spun around, and immediately walked towards her. "The bastards, they're tryin' to take my land."

"Huh?"

"That damn sheriff, he stopped by this mornin', told me I owe back taxes and that they need to be paid by next week or I lose my farm."

Seeing he was distraught and emotional, Helen caressed his upper arm and calmly said, "You're upset. Let's talk about this inside."

"Damn right I'm upset. They're trying to take my farm away from me!"

"Come inside. Let me make you a cup of tea," Helen said softly.

"Helen, I didn't come here for tea or to have you nod as I tell you my woes. I came here to see if you'd pay what you owe for that hundred acres now and to see if I can borrow the rest. I'll pay ya back. You know I'm good for it."

"Slow down. Your words are all bunching up."

Daniel took a deep breath and repeated what he'd just told her.

She thought about his offer and the dilemma he was in; it bothered her, but she didn't have that much cash reserves. "I can pay you for the land today, that's not a problem; but the loan, I'm not sure."

"Why not?"

"How about we start with how much you need?" Helen said.

"Eight hundred and seventeen dollars," Daniel answered as he pulled a handkerchief from his pocket and wiped his brow and face.

Shocked by the large amount, she looked down and thought of how she could make something happen for him. Her issue was if she took all the available cash she had, she could manage to help him, but it would leave her broke. It was a position she couldn't put herself in during the winter months. She'd need that money and then some, as spring would follow and she'd need to hire her farm hands for the season.

"Well, can you help me?" Daniel asked, his tone softening.

"I'm afraid I can't with the loan. It would leave me cash poor and unable—"

"I see what this is," Daniel said, a tinge of hatred coming through in his words.

"See what?" Helen asked.

"I heard rumors you and the sheriff were friendly and all. Is this a sick scheme, a deviant and twisted way to get my land for pennies on the dollar?" Daniel asked.

"Absolutely not, and those rumors are just that— rumors. I don't want anything to do with that man," Helen shot back, her voice rising in volume. She could only assume his accusation was coming from desperation. Here before her was a man about to lose everything he'd ever known.

"If not that, then this has to do with my son. I'm still suffering the consequences of his foolish actions," Daniel spat, referring to his son collaborating with Pinkerton agents a couple of years ago. That collaboration had resulted in the death of a young James family member and the maiming of Frank and Jesse's mother. Daniel's son ended up dead less than a year later, no doubt at the hand of a James sympathizer.

"Your son's actions don't speak for the father. What he did bears no weight on whether I can loan you the money or not," Helen said adamantly.

Daniel's eyes began to well up, but he fought back the tears. He turned away from her and asked, "When can I get the money for the hundred acres?"

"I'll have it later today. You have to come back anyway to sign the documents, as the notary will be here then," she said, reminding him.

"Very well," he said and walked off towards Alice.

"Daniel, please believe me when I tell you that if I had the money, I'd lend it to you," Helen said.

Unable to respond, he raised his hand and waved. He mounted Alice and rode off.

Helen's heart ached for Daniel. She knew well the emotional suffering of ruinous finances and felt fortunate that the fire had destroyed the records of her tax exemption.

"Finished another," Gabriel cried out with joy.

Hearing Gabriel's cheerful voice brought her comfort. Here was a boy who had lost so much but woke each morning happy to be alive. Yes, she knew many would say he did so because he was simple, but she found a lesson to be learned. Life was hard, very hard; but things could always be worse. Did she have complaints? Of course, and before Daniel arrived, she could have recited a few, but after seeing Daniel and the despair he was experiencing, she soon regarded her problems as not that bad.

"On to the next one," Gabriel hollered out. "Hurry up and help me."

"Coming," she said.

## ST. JOSEPH, MISSOURI

Graham entered his office and tossed his jacket on a chair. The high from his encounter with Daniel left him feeling both exhilarated and fearful. He wasn't a man of action, not in the physical sense. He'd never been an athletic man, nor could he be described as a gunman; but he wasn't afraid of using the system to destroy people, and that was exactly what he was going to do to Daniel. Long he'd suffered the arrows of disrespect, but now he was the sheriff, he wasn't going to just allow someone to say such things and get away with it. Too nervous to sit down, he paced and concocted a plan that would ensure Daniel would suffer the maximum pain.

The door to his office swung open.

He stopped and looked to see who it was. At first he thought it was Byron, as they had an appointment, but the stature of the man who engulfed the doorway told him it wasn't.

The morning's light cast through behind the man, making it hard to make out any discernable features.

"Can I help you?" Graham asked.

The shadowy figure walked farther into the office until he came into view. It was Frank Bradley; he was a massive man, standing a good eight inches taller than

Graham, with broad muscular shoulders and trunk-like arms. On his hip he had matching Smith & Wesson Model 3 Schofield revolvers with ivory grips. "Are you the sheriff?" Bradley asked.

Graham was intimidated instantly and felt small near the man. "Ah, yes."

"I'm looking for a couple of people, thought you'd be the best person to direct me to where I can find them," Bradley said.

"Oh, um, yes, I can help you. Please come sit down," Graham said, walking around his desk and taking a seat. He motioned for Bradley to sit, but he only stepped farther into the office and stood above the desk, towering like a giant, causing Graham's anxiety to grow. Graham found it hard to look into Bradley's steel-gray eyes, but forced himself to. Feigning confidence, Graham leaned back and asked, "So, who are you looking for?"

"A Michael McKinney and a Helen Mills," Bradley answered.

Graham sat forward and cleared his throat. "Um, Mike McKinney lives south of town, he owns a hog farm, and Helen Mills, um…who did you say you were?"

"How far out of town is McKinney?" Bradley asked.

"He lives past the lumber mill, has a few acres. You'll know you're close by the stench of hog shit," Graham answered.

"And the Mills woman?" Bradley asked.

"I'm sorry, sir, who are you?" Graham pressed.

"Name is Frank Bradley."

"And what do you want with these people?"

"That's my business. Now do you know where the Mills woman is?" Bradley asked.

"Listen here, Mr. Bradley, I don't know who you are, and I feel I may have made a mistake telling you where McKinney lives. How do I know you're not here to do these people harm?"

"I just have to ask them a few questions is all," Bradley replied.

"Who did you say you work for?" Graham asked.

"I work for myself," Bradley replied.

"Are you a marshal or something similar? 'Cause if you are, you might have some jurisdictional issues, being that I'm the sheriff of Buchanan County," Graham said.

Bradley sneered as he stared hard into Graham's eyes. He turned and began to walk towards the door, the floorboards creaking under each heavy footfall.

"Where are you going?" Graham asked, standing up.

"To go talk to Michael McKinney," Bradley replied.

Byron suddenly appeared in the doorway but stopped short of walking in when he saw Bradley coming. "Hi there," Byron said, his voice cracking.

Bradley paused and asked Byron, "Do you know where I can find Helen Mills?"

"Why yes, she lives a few miles south of town," Byron answered, giving Bradley all the details he knew about how to get to the Mills farm.

Bradley nodded and exited the office.

Byron raced inside, closed the door, and cried out, "Do you know who that is?"

"Yes, it's Frank Bradley," Graham answered as he

rushed past Byron to peer out the front door window.

"Not just Frank Bradley, it's Frank 'the Devil' Bradley. He's one of the most notorious bounty hunters this side of the Mississippi."

"A bounty hunter? What does he want with Helen?" Graham exclaimed.

"If he wants to see Helen, that can't be good," Byron said.

## MILLS FARM, ST. JOSEPH, MISSOURI

Taking Byron at his word concerning Bradley, Graham set off to warn Helen. He had his differences with her and even was scheming against her, but knowing she might get physically hurt by a strange man was where he drew the line.

Helen spotted him and met him before he could reach the house. This time she was prepared and held the Enfield rifle firmly in her hands.

Seeing she was armed, Graham pulled back on the reins hard. His horse came to a hard stop. "Helen, please don't shoot. I come in peace; I come to warn you."

Holding the rifle at the ready, she replied, "Warn me about what? That you're going to come after my farm like you did Daniel Askew's?"

Graham shook his head and answered, "What? No. Not that. I would never...no. Why would you say that?"

"He stopped by earlier, said you were putting his farm up for auction next week," Helen snapped.

"What's going on?" Gabriel said, walking up, a pair

of pliers in his hand.

"Gabriel, go into the house. Abigail is making lunch soon. Go get cleaned up," Helen ordered, her gaze still firmly on Graham, who hadn't dismounted his horse.

"Okay," Gabriel said. He waved at Graham and said, "Hi, Mr. Hooper."

"Well, hello, Gabriel."

Gabriel ran off and into the house.

"Helen, a man came into my office not long ago, a bounty hunter. He was asking about you," Graham blurted out, knowing he needed to get right to the point in order for her to listen.

"A bounty hunter? What does he want?" she asked, a look of shock washing across her face.

"I was hoping you'd be able to answer that. If you're in some sort of trouble, let me help you," Graham said. He was genuine in his offer to assist her, if this was how he could win her over, then he'd play the white knight.

"I haven't done anything wrong. There must be some sort of mistake," Helen said.

"This man, this bounty hunter, is a mean one. He's an unforgiving person. He'll hurt you. Let me protect you. Go get Gabriel, even grab Abigail, and come to my house. You'll be safe there."

"I'm not going anywhere with you. Whoever this bounty hunter is, he's made a mistake; I've done nothing wrong," Helen said.

"Please, Helen, listen to me," Graham urged.

Helen could see the visible worry on Graham's face. She could tell he was telling the truth, and this was what alarmed her. "If you think this bounty hunter will harm me, then stay and do your job as sheriff."

"I think it's best you all come with me," Graham again pressed. "This bounty hunter, he goes by the name Frank the Devil Bradley. He's a bad man, a very bad man."

"No, I won't leave. Let this bounty hunter come," Helen said as she motioned with the rifle. "And if he's such a bad man, why not arrest him?"

Frustrated with her tone, he barked at her, "Why won't you listen to me?"

"Funny, I feel the same about you," Helen quipped, referring to his relentless unsolicited romantic pursuit of her over the years.

Irritated by her stubbornness, he barked, "Fine, let it be known I warned you. What happens now is your fault." He pulled the reins hard, directing the horse to turn around.

"Goodbye, Sheriff," she snarled.

Graham stabbed his spurs into the horse's sides; seconds later the horse bolted forward.

Helen stayed glued to the spot until he was out of sight. Her mind swam with who this bounty hunter could be and what he could possibly want with her. Fear began to well up inside her; she knew many resented her success, specifically men who saw her as an interloper in the tobacco business. A woman's place was in the kitchen, not running a profitable tobacco farm. Not wanting to find out what the man was seeking, she raced inside and began to gather her things.

## ST. JOSEPH, MISSOURI

John tied his horse out front of the Western Union and made his way inside.

Inside, the distinct clicks of a message coming across filled the room. A young clerk sat behind the key and diligently wrote down what he was receiving. When the clicks stopped, the clerk put his pencil down and returned a message by depressing the key numerous times.

John patiently waited.

The clerk, neatly dressed, finished, turned and said, "Can I help you, sir?" He stood, straightened out his black vest and smoothed out his thin mustache.

"A message for John Nance?" John said.

"Yes, received it earlier today," the clerk said, pulling a folded piece of paper from a cubby and handing it to John.

John quickly opened it. On the yellowed paper one word was written: *CLOUDY*. Satisfied, he crumpled the paper in his hand and tossed it in a nearby trash can.

"Is that all, sir?" the clerk asked.

"Send one back to the sender, saying cloudy," John said.

The clerk scrunched his brow, looked outside, then shook his head. "Looks like a bluebird day."

"Commentary isn't welcome. Just send that, please."

"Yes, sir," the clerk said. "Anything else?"

"That's it," John said, taking a coin from his pocket and sliding it across the counter. "Keep the change." John wasn't surprised by the telegram. Garrett had only arrived recently; tracking Frank and Jesse down wouldn't happen that fast. The brothers had eluded the law for a long time; finding them in a day or two was doubtful.

"Thank you, sir," the clerk said with a beaming smile.

John exited the Western Union, looked left down the street, and spotted a sign emblazoned with one word, *BAR*. Having a drink sounded like a good idea, so he headed there.

He pushed the doors open and was greeted with the familiar smells of stale beer and fresh tobacco smoke. He looked around and found the bar was mostly empty. To his left sat several men playing a card game, and bellied up to the bar itself were three other men. The two-story establishment could easily handle ten times that number of patrons; John wondered where everyone was. He stepped up to the bar and waved to the bartender, who stood at the far end cleaning glassware.

"What can I get ya?" the bartender asked. He was an older man. If John were to guess, he was probably in his mid-fifties.

"Whiskey," John said.

The bartender grabbed a bottle and a shot glass from behind him and headed towards John. He walked with a noticeable limp.

John peered down and saw the man had a peg leg. "What happened?"

The bartender set the bottle and glass down and said, "Took a cannon ball to the knee at Shiloh."

"That must have hurt," John quipped.

The bartender poured the shot glass full, put the

cork back in the bottle, and replied, "You could say that. What I can't get over is the phantom leg feeling. It's very odd."

John had heard about that. It was a known syndrome where amputees could 'feel' the missing limb and even have pain. "Grab another glass. Drink is on me."

"No, thank you, quit drinking years ago. If you want, you can buy me a coffee," the bartender said.

"Sure, a coffee, then," John said.

The bartender returned with a steaming cup of coffee and raised it. "Thank you."

"To your missing leg," John said.

"What's your name?" the bartender asked.

"John Nance."

"You're new to these parts. Never seen ya before," the bartender said.

"Got here four days ago," John said before tossing back the shot.

"Where ya from?"

"All over," John said, deliberately keeping his answer vague. "You?"

"Born and raised in St. Joe, only left when the war broke out," the bartender replied, sipping his coffee slowly.

"Looks like a good place to be from," John said, pushing his glass closer with hopes the bartender would fill it.

Picking up on the cue, the bartender filled John's glass and asked, "What brings you here?"

"Work."

"Like what?"

"Field hand."

"Whose farm you working on?" the bartender asked.

"The Askew farm," John answered, picking up his glass.

"You're working for Daniel Askew?" the bartender asked, raising an eyebrow.

Seeing his question was pointed, John paused from taking a drink and replied with a question. "Is something wrong with that?"

"On account that his family are rat bastards," the bartender seethed.

"What makes you say that?" John asked, although he knew the answer.

The bartender leaned in close, his face now inches from John's, and whispered, "You watch yourself with that old man. He's trouble. His son was trouble, and it got him killed. If I were you, I'd go find work somewhere else."

"He pays good, and I need the work. What am I supposed to do?" John said.

"You just be careful. That family has been causing trouble for years. Now I hear the old man is going to lose his farm," the bartender said, standing back up. He took the bottle from in front of John and placed it back behind the bar.

"He's losing the farm?" John asked, feigning ignorance. He was shocked the word had spread so quickly.

"Yep, heard just a bit ago. Old man can't pay his

back taxes. Serves him right," the bartender said.

"What did his son do that was so bad?" John asked.

"Let's just say you don't cross certain people in these parts. Even if you don't like them, best to keep your damn mouth shut."

John drank the shot and put the glass down. "Is the bar closed to me?"

"For now. Not sure what kinda drinker you are. Last thing I want is for you to be shootin' your mouth off in here," the bartender warned.

"Just one more, c'mon," John urged.

"It's nothing personal. I'm just lookin' out for ya."

John slid the glass towards him and said, "If you're looking out for me, how about telling me what I should or shouldn't be talking about."

The bartender looked around to see if anyone was watching before leaning back in close and whispering, "Old man Askew's son snitched on the James family. It got a child killed and maimed their mother. Poor old girl lost her arm. Many like the James family around here 'cause they're still keepin' the fight goin' against those Yankee invaders, and others don't care for them, but keep their mouths shut 'cause they don't want to get lead poisoning, if you know what I mean."

"I know what you mean, but can I ask you a question?"

The bartender nodded.

"I thought the James family moved and aren't around here anymore," John said.

"I'll say this once, just assume they're here."

"Oh, I heard they were in Tennessee," John said.

The bartender leaned back and cocked his head. "I see for four days you've already heard a lot."

"I overheard a fella on the train talking the day I arrived," John lied.

"People are fools. Best not be talking about them. You never know who you're talking to," the bartender said.

The bartender's warning sounded identical to Daniel's. Fear ran deep in the locals as it pertained to the James family. They had scared them enough to keep people from talking or siding against them. It was a successful campaign of terror that reaped benefits for them.

"I'll take your advice. I'll just assume they're still here and keep to myself," John said.

The bartender winked and said, "Good man." He reached back and grabbed the bottle. "One more?"

"I thought you'd never ask," John quipped.

## ASKEW FARM, ST. JOSEPH, MISSOURI

With few options, Helen took Gabriel and Abigail to the one place no one would look for her and to a place she could leverage her stay: Daniel Askew's farm.

At first Daniel rebuffed her, but once she offered him the money to pay off his tax lien, he accepted her into his house with open arms.

When John returned from town, he was shocked to find her there and quickly began to ask detailed questions.

"Please tell me everything that the sheriff told you," John said.

Helen quickly brushed him off with the same reply she'd been giving him from the second he saw her at the house. "I don't want to involve you in this."

"You're here at Daniel's house. If someone comes looking for you here, I will be involved."

"This isn't your concern," she replied.

Daniel came into the room and took a seat. He pulled out his corncob pipe and packed it.

John gave him a look and said, "What's going on?"

Daniel lit the pipe and puffed. He blew a smoke ring and replied, "Mrs. Mills said she didn't want ya to know, then ya don't get to know."

All Helen had said was someone might be out to hurt her and that the sheriff had come to warn her. This wasn't enough for John; he again pressed, "If you don't tell me, I'll ride into town and ask the sheriff myself."

"You wouldn't dare," Helen said.

John stood and said, "Try me."

"Don't be a damn fool and get all hot-blooded. This ain't your business, so stay out of it."

"And it's yours?" John asked.

"Bein' that she's in my house, yeah, I say it's my business," Daniel snorted. "And don't lose your place, son; you're nuttin' but a worker, a damn field hand."

Insulted and annoyed, John exited the house.

"Where ya goin'?" Daniel asked.

"What do you like to say? None of your business," John shot back.

Helen followed him onto the front porch to make sure he wasn't headed for town. She found him pacing the front yard.

"I can help if you let me," John said.

She touched his arm and softly said, "I fear my past is coming back to haunt me, and I don't want you to get hurt."

He faced her and passionately said, "If that man comes here, I won't just do nothing. He'll have to come through me to get you; so you may not want to tell me for fear I'd get hurt, but I'm fighting for you whether I know what's going on or not."

Frustrated, she looked down and pondered her situation.

He lifted her head up and gazed into her deep blue eyes. "If you're thinking I'm just a mere field hand, you're wrong. I've done a lot in my life, I've been a soldier, a hired gun and a lawman; I can help. If I knew what was going on, I might be able to bring my experience to bear."

She tore her gaze away and walked off. She stopped and stared out across the rolling hills.

He came up behind her and said, "Please let me help you."

"A bounty hunter is looking for me," Helen said.

"For what? You have a bounty on your head?" John asked, shocked to hear this.

"I don't think so, but…"

"But what?"

Helen sighed and held her head low in shame. "Years

ago I received some money..." she said and again paused without finishing her thought.

"What kind of money? From whom?"

"My husband fought alongside William Quantrill during the war," she said.

"I knew that. What does the war and who your husband fought for have to do with a bounty hunter being here to track you down?" John asked, stepping in front of her.

"Quantrill and his men, the Raiders, fought differently than normal soldiers; they'd raid and rob shipments, and well..." she explained before taking a long sigh.

Seeing where the story was going, he said, "Your husband and Quantrill robbed someone notable or took something that someone wants back?"

"Maybe."

"What was it?"

Helen walked farther into the front yard. She was finding it hard to tell her secret to John.

He followed her and said, "You've said enough. No need to tell me more. So you think this bounty hunter has tracked this thing of value to you?"

"What else would he want with me?"

"I suppose you're right to be suspicious, but do you think he may want information on something else?"

"I'm a widow. I own a tobacco farm. I'm no one," she blurted out.

"You're a successful farmer and you're not a no one. Could one of the others who was in on the robbery be doing this?" John asked.

"No, that would never happen. They'd never rat me out, ever," Helen said confidently.

"How can you be so sure?"

"'Cause I know. There were six men involved. Two men died in the guerilla fighting after the war, one of them was my husband, and the other four—two I know would never give me up. I suppose the others might, but I doubt it," Helen said, her mind contemplating the possibilities.

"Are the other four alive, do you know?" he asked.

"They're alive."

"If they're still alive, then there's a chance one of them gave your name to this bounty hunter," John said.

Helen rested her face in her hand and sighed loudly.

Seeing the stress wear on her, he put his hands tenderly on her shoulders and said, "I swear no harm will come to you."

"Why would you risk your life to protect me and Gabriel? You don't know me. Trust me when I say you don't want this trouble."

"Let me be the one who decides what I want," John said.

Believing him, she laid her head against his chest. "Thank you."

"Have you told Daniel?"

"No."

"What about the sheriff?" John asked.

"God no, no one except the other four, you, and this bounty hunter knows anything about this," Helen said.

"Speaking of the bounty hunter, would you happen to know his name?" John asked.

"The sheriff said his name was, oh gosh, I can't quite remember...wait, he said something about the Devil."

John's eyes widened, as he'd heard about Bradley before.

"That look, what's that look?" Helen asked, noticing John's expression shifted on his face.

Not wanting to concern her, he lied, "I'm just thinking."

"Have you heard about him before?" she asked, referring to Bradley.

"I have."

"The sheriff said he was an evil man. Is that true?"

"I've lived long enough to know that any man can be evil, so we should take this seriously," John replied.

# CHAPTER FOUR

"Sooner or later everyone sits down to a banquet of consequences." – Robert Louis Stevenson

## MCKINNEY FARM, SOUTH OF ST. JOSEPH, MISSOURI

## NOVEMBER 8, 1876

Graham woke needing to know what had become of McKinney and Helen. Leaving at first light, he rode with two deputies directly to Helen's house, but found it vacant, and by the looks of it, someone had been there looking too. The rooms of the house were torn apart. Obviously Bradley wasn't just looking for them but for something they had, but what? He searched high and low for them across the farm but couldn't find them. Either Bradley had taken them, or they had gone into hiding. With nothing to go on, they departed and went to the McKinney farm; there they found a similar scene with one exception: in the barn they found McKinney, alive but badly beaten.

"What happened? Who did this to you?" Graham asked.

"I fell down," McKinney said, loading up a bucket of grain.

"With Frank Bradley? Did he do this to you?" Graham pressed.

McKinney pushed past Graham and exited the barn, headed for the hog pen.

Graham followed and kept asking questions, which McKinney ignored. Losing patience, Graham grabbed him by the shoulder and turned him around. "Damn it, Mike, tell me what happened."

"Listen, Sheriff, I had a bad fall is all. Now please leave my farm; go," McKinney said.

"Frank Bradley came to my office yesterday, and he specifically asked for you and Helen Mills. I went to the Mills farm, and it was trashed, torn up; she's missing. I come here, and your house looks like hers, and I find you badly beaten up. Yet you're going to tell me everything here and your injuries have nothing to do with Frank Bradley?"

"Nothing, I don't even know the man," McKinney growled in anger. "Sheriff, leave my farm; go. I simply fell down. I'm getting clumsy in my old age."

"Damn it, Mike, if that bounty hunter has threatened you, I can help. I'm the law around here," Graham declared.

"Can't a man fall down and hurt himself without being interrogated?" McKinney complained.

"And your house, what happened in there?" Graham asked.

"I misplaced something," McKinney replied.

"Must have been important to turn the place upside down," Graham quipped.

"It was," McKinney said before shaking his head in frustration.

"What?" Graham asked, confused by the head movement.

"Nothing, now go, please," McKinney urged, his eyes darting around.

Noticing his wandering eyes, Graham looked around and asked, "Are you waiting for someone or fearful someone is watching you?"

McKinney turned around and rushed off towards the hog pen again, ignoring Graham's question.

Seeing McKinney wasn't going to cooperate, Graham gave up. "If you change your mind, you know where to find me."

"Goodbye, Sheriff." McKinney waved.

"Now what?" Fowler, one of his deputies, asked, pulling his horse close.

"We keep looking for the widow Mills, that's what we do," Graham said.

"What about Frank Bradley? Should we arrest him and bring him in?" Lee, the other deputy, asked after mounting his horse.

"Arrest him for what?" Graham replied.

Lee and Fowler gave each other a curious look. Lee answered, "Bring him in for questioning. He's clearly involved here."

Graham knew what Lee was asking was right, but going after Bradley opened the door for a violent encounter. It was something he wasn't prepared for.

"Sheriff, Deputy Lee is right," Fowler said.

Knowing he had to lead by example, if he failed to at the minimum speak with Bradley, he'd be what he was often called: a coward.

## ASKEW FARM, ST. JOSEPH, MISSOURI

John woke to the smell of bacon wafting through his bedroom. The aroma made his stomach growl and his mouth water. Unable to stop the hunger pangs, he got dressed quickly and raced downstairs. In the kitchen he found Abigail cooking.

"Take a seat, sir. I'll have breakfast on the table in a jiffy," she said.

"Smells great, and is that biscuits too?" John asked, seeing a baking sheet filled with three rows of browned biscuits.

"Why yes, it is, my very own recipe too, sir," Abigail answered with a broad smile.

John went to the dining room and took a seat. He could hardly wait to devour the food.

Daniel walked into the room and took his seat at the head of the table. He gave John a hard look and said, "It's nice havin' someone else cook."

"I bet it is," John said.

"Tell me, what did Mrs. Mills tell you last night? You two spent a considerable amount of time outside. Did she tell you what that bounty hunter wants?"

"Not exactly," John answered honestly.

"What did she say…exactly?" Daniel pried.

"I'm not sure I'm at liberty to divulge what she told me in confidence," John said.

"You work for me, son. Now tell me," Daniel

snapped.

Helen entered the room and fired back, "I appreciate your hospitality, but it is coming at a price that I've already agreed to pay."

"It's only fair you tell me specifically why you're in my house," Daniel said.

"I'd rather not; too many people know as it is. What you need to know, Mr. Askew, is that I appreciate you opening your house to me, Gabriel and Abigail; and the deal we made had nothing to do with knowing my business. If you're changing the terms of our mutually agreed situation, then consider it null and void," Helen said sternly.

Daniel grimaced and said, "Fine, I don't really care. Am I getting my money tomorrow like you promised?"

"Yes," Helen answered.

"Good."

Abigail appeared with a tray full of food. She placed it on the table and took a seat next to Helen.

Daniel raised his brows and groaned, "No, her kind don't sit at my table."

Shocked, Helen snapped, "She eats with me at home, and she'll eat with me here."

"You might do that in your house, but not mine," Daniel argued.

"Daniel, it's not a big deal," John said.

"You shut your mouth, boy. You're mistaking your place all too often now. And if you think I'll let you seat your house slave at my table and eat, you're mistaken, Mrs. Mills," Daniel said.

"I'm not a house slave no more. No, I'm a free woman," Abigail declared, her head held high.

"You're a damn blackie, and you won't be sitting at my table," Daniel shot back.

Helen stood up, gave Abigail and look, and said, "Let's go eat in the kitchen."

John watched them both leave the dining room. When the door swung closed, he cocked his head at Daniel and asked, "Was that necessary?"

"My house, my rules," Daniel roared.

John stood with his plate in his hand and marched into the kitchen, leaving Daniel alone in the dining room.

Seeing John, Helen said, "You didn't need to do that."

"I did what was right," John said, sitting next to Abigail. "The food smells amazing. Thank you for making it."

"You're welcome, sir," Abigail said.

"No need to call me sir. Please call me John."

"Very well, you're welcome, John."

"Abigail and I have been through hell and back. Our relationship has changed over the years. She first came to me as my property, but after she was emancipated and decided to stay, we grew closer and closer. If I had to describe her, I'd say she's my best friend," Helen said.

"The feeling is mutual," Abigail said. She gave John a look and asked, "You're a Southern man; how many slaves did you own?"

"Zero. I was a tenant farmer. I worked my own land," John said proudly.

The kitchen door swung open, and Daniel stood in the doorway. He grimaced and said, "Get yer assess in here, including you." He pointed at Abigail.

Helen looked at Abigail for her approval. She nodded.

The trio joined Daniel in the dining room.

"Where's Gabriel?" John asked, finally noticing he was absent.

"He said he wasn't feeling well, so he's still lying in bed resting," Helen explained.

"Stomach?" John asked.

"Achy," Helen replied, scooping up a forkful of eggs.

Hearing that concerned John. The last person he knew who complained of being achy had died weeks later from smallpox. After breakfast, he went to the bedroom where Gabriel was sleeping. He saw the door was cracked open and peeked in. There he saw Helen sitting next to him, caressing his cheek.

Gabriel saw John and called out, "Morning, John."

Feeling as if he'd just been caught spying, he nervously said, "Oh, good morning. I heard you weren't feeling well, thought I'd come up and check on you. I see you're in good hands though."

"I'm fine, just need to rest," Gabriel said with a big smile.

"Good, glad to hear it. I'll let you get back to it, then," John said then headed back downstairs. He exited the house and stood on the porch just in time to see a rider heading their way.

Daniel had seen the rider too and knew exactly who

it was. He walked out of the house with his shotgun in his hand. "Damn son of a bitch, I guess he wants some lead in his belly."

"I don't think he's coming to see you," John said, guessing Graham was coming with two deputies in tow to see if Helen was there.

Graham, accompanied by Lee and Fowler, rode up but didn't dismount. "Good morning, Mr. Askew," Graham said, tipping his hat.

Daniel raised the barrel of his shotgun and barked, "I thought I told you not to come back."

"I'm here on different business," Graham replied.

Lee and Fowler slowly walked their right hands back towards their pistols, unsure if Daniel was going to shoot.

"I'm looking for Mrs. Mills. Do you happen to know where she might be?" Graham asked.

"Get outta here!" Daniel roared.

"Goddamn it, Daniel, I'm here to make sure the widow Mills and her nephew are okay. There's a man pursuing them. It appears he might have hurt McKinney, and all I'm doing is trying to protect her from that same fate or worse. I'm concerned for her safety."

John didn't know how to answer, so he remained quiet.

"You can call off your auction. I'll have the money to pay those damn taxes in a couple of days," Daniel shouted.

Shocked to hear it, Graham asked, "So you came into some money, did you?"

"None of yer business how I got the money. Just

know you rat bastards aren't gettin' my land," Daniel crowed.

"Good for you. Now can you answer my question? Have you seen Mrs. Mills, or do you know where she is?" Graham asked.

Daniel remained quiet.

Graham turned to John and asked, "And you? Do you know anything?"

John shook his head.

Graham gritted his teeth and decided to get more aggressive. "Mind if I look inside?"

"Over my dead body," Daniel replied, leaning forward with the shotgun now in his shoulder.

"You know something, Daniel, you're a mean old bastard," Graham said.

"That's the first thing you've said I agree with. Now get, be gone; there ain't nothin' here for ya," Daniel barked.

"Helen, if you're here, let me help!" Graham hollered

Helen heard the shouting and came to the window. She peeked out through the linen curtains, ensuring she didn't show herself. She wasn't about to let Graham know she was there. She didn't trust him one bit, even though he was probably right, and being with him would add a layer of protection.

Graham carefully looked at each window, hoping he'd spot her but didn't. He then set his eyes on Daniel and said, "If you see her, send someone to tell me. The man who's after her is not to be taken lightly."

"Get!" Daniel snapped.

Graham pulled the reins of his horse and turned around. "C'mon, you two, let's keep looking for her."

The trio bolted away as fast as they'd arrived and disappeared over the rolling hills.

Helen emerged from the house and said, "Thank you, Daniel."

"Lyin' to the law wasn't part of the deal, but thankfully for you I enjoyed it," Daniel said, walking past her and into the house.

John approached and said, "We need to be prepared for this."

"Maybe I should leave, head to Kentucky; I have cousins there," she said.

"Or maybe instead of waiting for him to find you, we go find him and end this," John said.

## ST. JOSEPH, MISSOURI

Graham, Lee and Fowler spent the greater part of the day trying to locate Helen after being misled at the Askew farm. Tired and in need of a good meal, they rode back into town for nourishment and a few drinks. Without debate they chose to go to the Great Ox, a popular restaurant.

After devouring their food and more than a few beverages, Lee and Fowler left for home. The plan was to continue searching for her the next day.

Graham, however, decided to stay and continue drinking at the bar.

"Sheriff Hooper, there you are," Byron said loudly,

walking up behind Graham, who was leaning against the bar, a shot glass in his hand.

"Hi, Byron," Graham said, tossing the drink back. He slammed it on the bar and motioned for the bartender to fill it. "Want a drink?"

"Ah, sure," Byron said, pointing towards the whiskey bottle.

The bartender set another glass down and filled both. "Do you want the bottle?" he asked Graham.

"Yeah, keep it here," Graham answered, his words beginning to slur from too much to drink.

"Sheriff, you're looking a bit tipsy," Byron quipped.

"Tipsy? Who uses that word? Women and kept men," Graham snarked.

Shocked by his reply, Byron chose not to reply and instead asked, "Where have you been all day? We had a meeting to finalize the list of liens you need to serve."

"I had more pressing issues, law enforcement, life-and-death issues," Graham answered with a condescending tone.

Known in town as a nosey busybody, Byron couldn't resist finding out what was really happening. "What's this life-and-death issue?"

"Michael McKinney, I saw him today. He was black and blue all over," Graham replied.

"Oh my Lord," Byron gasped. He looked around to ensure no one was eavesdropping. Seeing he could speak freely, he asked, "It was Devil Bradley, wasn't it?"

"I can only assume."

"And the widow Mills, is she fine?" Byron asked.

"Not sure, I can't find her. Her house was ransacked, but I didn't find any evidence she'd been hurt. I spent the entire day's light looking for her."

"Do you suppose Bradley kidnapped her?" Byron asked.

A drunk patron bumped into Graham. "Excuse me."

Perturbed, Graham turned around and shoved the man. "Watch where you're going!"

The man apologized and stumbled off.

Having never seen Graham act this way, Byron pressed forward with his curious questions. "If she's not been taken, then where could she be?"

"I gave her a heads-up that Bradley was looking for her. She acted as if she wasn't concerned, but I don't think he took her. I think she must have heeded my warning and left. I went to the Askew farm, thinking that she might go there, but he told me she wasn't there…I don't know, something seems off."

"What do you mean?" Byron asked, leaning in closer.

"Daniel told me he has the money to pay off the lien. Where did he get it from? She goes missing and suddenly he has the money. If I were to guess, she's gone to his farm and is hiding out."

"Oh, I see, she paid him to hide her and the retarded nephew. Makes sense."

"It does. I wouldn't think that, but he suddenly has the money for the lien, but of course, I could be wrong," Graham said, his words becoming more slurred. He picked up his glass, spilled a bit, then tossed it back.

"Can we meet tomorrow to go over that final lien

list?" Byron asked.

"Can't, heading out at first light to continue looking for her," Graham said.

"And what about Bradley? I hear he's staying over at the Blossom Hotel. You going to arrest him?" Byron asked.

"Why does everyone keep asking me that? I'm thinking about it, but I don't have any evidence, and I won't risk a damn gunfight with a man who's a known gunman. I'll go after him when I have something solid, not just coincidence," Graham snapped.

"You're just thinking about it? You're the sheriff and you think he hurt McKinney and possibly kidnapped Helen. Do I need to remind you of your job?" Byron jabbed.

Graham stood erect and in a fit of anger pushed Byron hard. "Are you calling me a coward? Huh? I don't know for sure he's done anything, and you want me to just go over there and arrest him? How about I deputize you and send you over there?"

"First thing I'll remind you of is I'm not the sheriff, you are. And second, I'm not calling you a coward, I'm merely asking if you were because things seem to point to him. At least go speak to him," Byron said.

Graham got into Byron's face and hollered, spit raining down on Byron's face. "Will everyone stop telling me how to do my job!"

"The man is over at the Blossom Hotel now. At least go over and talk to him," Byron shouted back.

The entire bar grew quiet, and all eyes focused on

them.

"If you or another person calls me a coward, I'll shoot you dead," Graham said, pulling his pistol from his holster and placing it against Byron's forehead. "Call me a coward, do it!"

"Graham, you've lost your senses. This isn't you. I didn't call you a coward. Don't put words in my mouth. Put the gun down and let's talk about this," Byron pleaded, his hands raised and trembling.

"For far too long people have called me a coward. I'm not, not one bit. And now you, a man I called friend, coming in here and saying I'm one. How dare you?" Graham roared.

"I wasn't calling you a coward, I swear. I was merely—"

"Shut up!" Graham screamed, uncocking the pistol and placing it back in the holster. "Go. Leave me alone. I'll deal with that bounty hunter soon enough."

"But—" Byron said in a weak attempt to counter but was cut off.

"Leave while you can still walk out of here," Graham shouted.

Byron didn't say another word. He bolted towards the exit and left.

Graham looked around the bar and hollered, "Mind your own damn business."

The bartender, a large and sturdy man, stepped up and whispered, "Sheriff, you're upset. How about you call it a night?"

Graham gave him a hard look, but the bartender

didn't flinch.

"You'll thank me in the morning, trust me," the bartender said, giving him a wink.

Graham thought and came to the same conclusion. "How much do I owe you?"

"We'll settle up another time. Go home and get some rest," the bartender said.

Graham nodded and stumbled out of the bar, knocking over chairs and brushing by patrons. Outside, he leaned up against a stanchion to steady himself. Seeing the moon just above the eastern horizon, he stared into it and said, "Where are you, Helen?"

# CHAPTER FIVE

"Sooner or later everyone sits down to a banquet of consequences." – Robert Louis Stevenson

## ST. JOSEPH, MISSOURI

## NOVEMBER 9, 1876

Lured by the smell of eggs and bacon, Bradley stepped into the dining room of the hotel. Heads and eyes all snapped in his direction. Enjoying the attention, he made sure to make eye contact with each person, taking glee as they shyly looked away. He approached the first table available and sat, making sure his back was towards the wall.

A young waitress approached and asked, "Coffee?"

"Yes, and I'll take three eggs, bacon and toast."

"Coming right up," the waitress said and hurried off. She quickly returned with a steaming cup of coffee and placed it in front of him.

Bradley nodded and picked up the hot coffee and took a sip. Out of nowhere, Byron walked up and stopped feet from him.

"Excuse me, Mr. Bradley," Byron asked.

Bradley cut his eyes at Byron and asked, "What do you want?"

Byron held out his hand and said, "Byron James, Buchanan County commissioner, at your service."

Bradley rolled his eyes and again said, "I'm enjoying my coffee, and I tend to enjoy it more alone."

"May I sit?" Byron asked.

"No."

"Sir, if you'll allow me, I have a proposition for you, one that will be lucrative if you'll let me sit and explain it to you," Byron said nervously.

Bradley grunted and said, "Hurry up."

Byron pulled out the opposite chair and sat down. "Thank you."

The waitress reappeared and placed his plate of food in front of him. "There you go." She looked at Byron and asked, "Will you be needing anything, sir?"

"He don't want nothin'. Now go away," Bradley said, waving the waitress away.

Startled, she turned and raced off.

"You've got until I finish my food," Bradley said and began eating, stabbing his food aggressively and shoving it into his wide mouth.

Seeing he didn't have much time, as Bradley was plowing through the plate quickly, he said, "Ah, well, you see, I know you are a man for hire. I know you're here looking for Helen Mills…."

Hearing her name, Bradley stopped eating. Yolk dripped down from his chin and onto his stubbled chin. "You know where she is?"

"Well, if I were to say yes, what could I get for that information?" Byron asked, leaning in closer.

Bradley leaned in and returned his question with one. "How about me not killing you, will that be enough?"

Byron gulped and sat back in his chair.

Happy that he'd frightened Byron, Bradley chuckled and said, "You scare easily."

"You're a man with quite the reputation for violence," Byron said in his defense.

Using his sleeve to wipe his face, Bradley asked, "You know where this Mills woman is?"

"I believe I might," Byron said.

"I normally don't pay for information, but on account I want to wrap this job up quickly, I'm willing to reconsider my usual business practices," Bradley said.

"Shall we go to my office and conclude this?" Byron asked.

"I don't have time for that. What do you want for this information?" Bradley asked.

"One thousand dollars," Byron replied, his voice cracking slightly.

Bradley rolled his eyes and went back to eating without giving Byron a reply.

A lengthy pause made Byron worried. He sat and watched as Bradley ate and began to feel he might have asked for too much. "Seven hundred and fifty?"

Bradley didn't respond, nor did he look up; instead he tore a piece from the toast and used it to mop up the yolk and grease on his plate.

Sweat formed on Byron's brow and upper lip. He removed his handkerchief and dabbed both areas. "Five hundred, final offer," he said, feigning confidence.

Still, Bradley remained stoic. He tossed back the remaining coffee, slammed the cup on the table, and reached into his pocket and pulled out a few coins. He fished through until he found the one he wanted and placed it on the table. Never making eye contact with Byron, he stood and marched off towards the exit.

Concern grew to panic; Byron jumped to his feet and chased after Bradley.

Bradley stepped onto the front walkway of the hotel and took a deep breath.

"Three hundred?" Byron asked, stepping up next to Bradley, his head two inches shorter than Bradley's hulking shoulders.

"The air smells good in this town; I like it here. Maybe I'll come back once I'm done with this job," Bradley said.

"Ah, yes, this is a nice town. Um, do we have a deal?" Byron asked.

"You said you might know where she is. Either you know or don't know. Like I said, I don't normally pay for information, but if I have to, the person selling better know for sure 'cause if they don't, I'll come lookin' for my money back, and you don't want that."

Byron now questioned what he was doing, but he was a betting man, even willing to go as far as bet with a man who was a notorious killer. "I feel my information is correct."

"I don't like feelings much. Either you know or don't know, period," Bradley said and stepped off the walkway and into the street.

Not wanting to let any amount of money go, Byron blurted out, "I know, I know." He ran up to Bradley and repeated, "I know, I know where she is."

Bradley reached into his pocket and pulled out a roll of paper money. He peeled off two bills and handed it to Byron. "Two hundred, now where is she?"

\*\*\*

Graham rubbed his head to alleviate the throbbing his hangover was giving him. It took a lot of effort for him to rise that morning and get to the office. If it weren't for Helen, he'd no doubt have still been in bed nursing his ailments.

The door of the office swung open and slammed. "Sheriff!" Deputy Fowler hollered, catching his breath.

Ignoring him, Graham sat at his desk, head in hand.

Lee, on the other hand, jumped to his feet.

Fowler ran up to Graham and howled, "Sheriff, I just saw the bounty hunter. He's at the livery."

Graham lifted his head and said, "No doubt going back out to look for Helen."

"Don't you think—" Fowler asked but was interrupted.

"If you mutter one more thing, I'll fire you. You understand?" Graham roared. He got to his feet, steadied himself, grabbed his jacket, and headed for the door. "Lee, man the office."

Lee groaned and plopped back in his chair, his face drooping with disappointment.

Fowler kept his mouth shut. The last thing he needed was to lose his job. Like a puppy with his tail between his legs, he followed Graham out the door and down the street towards the livery.

With each step Graham took, he prayed the encounter wasn't going to go badly, but there was no going back because not going and confronting Bradley had worse consequences.

Just as they approached the main entrance, Bradley trotted out on the back of his horse. He gave Graham a second's look and smiled. "Howdy, Sheriff."

"Mr. Bradley, I need to ask you a few questions," Graham said sternly.

Fowler fell in just behind Graham at his five o'clock.

Bradley sized them both up with a quick glance. He turned his horse and faced them directly. "What's with everyone wanting to talk to me this morning?"

Graham furrowed his brow, confused by the comment; he quickly ignored it and asked, "I saw Michael McKinney yesterday. He's not looking good; it appears someone beat him up."

"Is that so?" Bradley quipped.

"Yes, and his house as well as the Mills house were torn apart, like someone was looking for something. Was that you?" Graham asked, deliberately slowing the tempo of how he spoke.

"Sheriff, I stopped by and spoke with Michael McKinney and went by the Mills house but don't know anything about tearing them apart. I only have a few questions to ask. McKinney was forthright; now I just need to find the Mills woman and ask her those same questions. Once I do that, I'll be on my way, although I do like it here," Bradley said, leaning on the horn of the saddle with both hands.

"You're claiming you don't know anything about what happened at their houses though you admit to being there?" Graham asked, knowing Bradley was lying but too afraid to call him out.

Fowler wasn't afraid, though, and belted out, "He's lyin', Sheriff. That son of a bitch is a liar!"

Bradley sat up and shifted in his saddle. He casually drew his right hand back towards his gun belt and said, "Boy, you'd best watch what you say."

Stunned by Fowler's outburst and not wanting this to turn into a violent gunfight, Graham scolded Fowler. "Shut your mouth. Let me deal with this!"

"Listen to the sheriff, boy," Bradley said.

Fowler gritted his teeth and returned Bradley's hard stare.

"Mr. Bradley, you have to admit, the situation with McKinney and Mills looks suspicious," Graham said in a diplomatic tone.

"I guess you could say that, but let me ask you, did McKinney finger me for what happened?" Bradley asked.

"No, he didn't, but I think he might be too afraid to tell me the truth," Graham said. "Tell me, do you know where widow Mills is?"

"I don't, but I'm hopin' to track her down soon. Like I said, I have a few questions that need to get answered."

"Mind if we ride along with you? I have a few questions for her as well," Graham asked, surprising himself with the bold proposal.

Bradley chuckled and replied, "I like to work alone, but if I find her, I'll be sure to pass along that you're looking for her. Now if this is all, I need to get going."

"That's all…for now," Graham said.

Bradley grinned and tipped his hat. "Good day, Sheriff." He pulled the horse's reins hard and bolted out of town at a full gallop.

"Sheriff, he's lyin'," Fowler complained.

"You think I don't know that? But we have no evidence, and McKinney isn't talking. What's your recommendation?"

"Arrest him," Fowler said.

"You're a good person, but naïve. Frank Bradley isn't a man who gets arrested. If you plan on being in this line of work for long, you need to know the difference between men like Bradley and others."

"We could have taken him," Fowler said, challenging Graham.

"Maybe or maybe not. If we're going to arrest him, we'll need more evidence and a plan that doesn't have us standing off against a man like that."

The youthful cockiness was hard for Fowler to let go. He fumed, "I think I could take him. He's old and probably slow."

"Fowler, just shut your mouth and go get our horses ready, including Lee's" Graham ordered.

"Where we goin'?"

"We're going to follow Bradley 'cause my gut tells me he knows where Helen is," Graham replied.

"But where are you going?" Fowler asked.

"To get more guns," Graham answered

## ASKEW FARM, ST. JOSEPH, MISSOURI

The morning was spent arguing over who would go with Helen to get the money to pay Daniel, with John winning out; he convinced Daniel that he was best to protect her along the way. All Daniel wanted was his money, and after much thought, he agreed that John was better equipped to protect her and bring it back.

Helen didn't like leaving Gabriel and Abigail behind, but Daniel convinced her that he'd let no one hurt them. It wasn't ideal, but taking them all with her wasn't a viable option either.

Helen was exhausted, emotionally and physically. She'd spent the greater part of the night tossing and turning. The idea of heading to Kentucky kept popping in her head, and each time it did, it made more and more sense to leave Missouri. It had been a long time since the anxiety and tension of the war years had visited her, and once it had come roaring back, it reminded her how unstable that time in her life was.

Out of an abundance of caution, John plotted a route that took them overland from the Askew farm into town. Helen agreed to the route, and the two set out.

Once they were out of sight of the Askew house, Helen cried out, "Stop, we need to stop."

John pulled his horse to a stop and asked, "What's wrong?"

"We're going the wrong way," she said, pulling her

horse to the left, or west.

"No, we're headed in the right direction. If we stay along this draw, we'll hit the stream. From there we'll—"

She interrupted him. "We're not going into town."

A look of shock swept across his face. "We're not?"

"No."

"Then where are we going?"

"Back to my farm, I have the money there," she said without further explanation before kicking the horse and sprinting off.

John grunted with frustration; he hated last minute changes, especially ones that tossed the entire plan out the window. But what was he to do? As she rode farther away, he had no choice but to follow, so he did just that.

## ST. JOSEPH, MISSOURI

Graham burst through his office door and hollered, "Get your stuff, Lee. We're heading out in pursuit of Bradley."

A broad smile stretched across Lee's face as he sprang to his feet like a jack-in-the-box.

Graham went directly to the gun rack, took three Winchester Model 73 rifles, and set them on the table next to it. Using a sack, he filled it with several boxes of ammunition for the rifles. Lee approached just in time for Graham to hand him the sack. Cradling the rifles, Graham said, "There might be a fight today. Are you ready?"

"Yes, Sheriff," Lee said, a look of excitement on his face.

"Good."

Just as the two were about to exit, the young clerk from the Western Union appeared.

"Sheriff, good morning, just the man I need to see," the clerk said with a toothy grin.

"I don't have time," Graham said, pushing past him.

"Oh, sorry, Sheriff, I was just dropping off a telegram," the clerk said, holding out a folded piece of paper.

Curious, Graham asked, "Who's it from?"

"A Mr. Chase in Kansas City, sir," the clerk replied, still holding the paper out in front of him.

"Here, give it to me," Graham snapped. "Lee, head to the livery and saddle up."

Lee bounded off.

The clerk's smile vanished, as he'd finally become aware that Graham was annoyed with him. He handed him the telegram and stood patiently waiting to see if Graham needed anything else.

Graham unfolded the paper. It read: *MISS HELEN MILLS DID SIGN TAX DEFERMENT IN SIXTY-SIX. I HAVE DOCUMENTATION IF NEEDED. – MR. CHASE, KANSAS CITY.*

Just a couple of days before, Graham would have been thrilled to receive this telegram. Now all he wanted to do was protect Helen from harm. He folded the paper and shoved it into his pocket.

"Shall I reply?" the clerk asked.

He thought for a few seconds and decided that having the information was valuable and could be used if he needed it. "Yes, say please send documentation to sheriff's office immediately. Any expenses will be reimbursed."

The clerk wrote the message down on a small pocket-sized notepad and replied, "I'll send this right away."

"Good, thank you," Graham said, rushing off.

"That will be forty cents," the clerk hollered after him.

"I'll pay you later. Go send the telegram," Graham replied, racing off towards the livery.

## ASKEW FARM, ST. JOSEPH, MISSOURI

Only when Daniel heard Abigail scream did he regret going to the north side of his farm to check the creek level. He shuffled back to his horse, Alice, as fast as his old legs could take him and mounted her. With a snap of the reins and a kick, Alice bolted towards the main house. Upon cresting a small hill, he spotted a large man dragging Abigail out of the house by her hair. His heart felt like it was going to pound out of his chest, and his muscles tensed. He kicked Alice harder so she'd run faster, but she was already going her top speed.

Bradley looked up when he heard the galloping coming towards him. He shoved Abigail to the side, drew one of his Schofield pistols, and leveled it at Daniel.

Seeing the gun drawn and fearing for his life, Daniel pulled back on the reins hard, causing Alice to rear violently, enough that he fell off, landing hard on the ground.

Using his left hand, Bradley drew his second Schofield and leveled it at Abigail. "You stay right there, sweetheart."

Daniel slowly got to his knees. He looked up to find the pistol still pointed at him. Just behind Bradley, he caught a glimpse of Abigail sobbing on the ground, her knees drawn to her chest. He raised his hands and said, "Listen here, I'm not sure what ya want, but whatever it is, I don't have it."

"Where is Helen Mills?" Bradley asked.

"I-I don't know," Daniel said with a stutter.

"I heard she was here. Tell me!" Bradley snarled, cocking the pistol in his left hand.

"Listen, mister, I don't know where she is. Ya might check at her house. She lives—" Daniel replied.

Bradley shook his head and said, "Why must everyone lie?" He squeezed off a shot from the pistol in his left hand. The bullet ricocheted off the ground next to Abigail.

Abigail scurried away, tears of fear flowing down her cheeks and mixing with the fresh blood on her lips and nose.

"Next bullet goes through her head," Bradley said, cocking the pistol again.

"Go ahead, shoot her. It won't change that I don't know where she is," Daniel said calmly, hoping the ruse would work.

Bradley cocked the pistol in his right hand and said, "How about you? How about I put one in that left shoulder?"

"Mister, listen, we don't know where Helen Mills is," Daniel pleaded, his hands still raised.

Bradley pulled the trigger, the bullet racing inches past Daniel's face. He cocked the pistol again and hollered, "Next one goes somewhere in ya."

Abigail managed to get on all fours. Her head bobbled as she rigidly moved until she lifted her arms off the ground and knelt. "Please, sir, don't do this. We're simple folk. We don't know nothin'."

"Are you the owner of this farm?" Bradley asked Daniel.

"Yes," Daniel simply replied.

"Then this woman here, she works for you?" Bradley asked.

"Yes."

"Is anyone else here? Anyone besides Helen Mills?" Bradley asked.

"No, sir, just me and her. I have a field hand, but he's in town gettin' some supplies," Daniel lied.

"So there's no one in the house, not a soul?" Bradley asked.

"No," Daniel answered.

"Good," Bradley said, uncocking the pistol in his left hand and holstering it. "You mind if I look around, then?"

"Go ahead. You won't find nothin'," Daniel said.

Bradley marched over, grabbed Daniel by the back of the neck, and lifted him to his feet. "You're coming with me." The two crossed the short distance from where they were and entered the house. Room by room, Bradley went with Daniel in his grip. Nowhere was there evidence of anyone or anything that could link Helen to the house. As they went to leave the house, Bradley spotted an oil lamp and got an idea. He took it and the box of matches next to it and exited the house, stopping on the front porch. "Is anyone hiding in the house? Somewhere not obvious?"

"I told ya no," Daniel said now more defiantly.

"Old man, I'm not someone to mess with. Do you understand?" Bradley snarled.

"There's no one else here. You can burn this place to the ground, but it won't change a damn thing, you hear me?"

"Very well," Bradley said, shoving Daniel off the porch.

Daniel collided with the ground hard, his face skidding off the gravel surface.

Bradley turned, swung the screen door wide, and smashed the glass oil lamp on the floor of the first room. He finally holstered his second pistol, took a match from the box, and held it high. "One last chance!"

Seeing what he was about to do, Abigail screamed, "There's someone in there. Don't do it, please, Lord, don't do it!"

A grin stretched across Bradley's face. He lowered the match, turned and asked, "Who's in the house?"

Abigail rushed to the base of the porch stairs and said, "Just a boy. He's simpleminded, means no harm. I've been taken care of him for years."

"Where is he?" Bradley asked.

"A trapdoor in the kitchen beneath the table, he's in there," Abigail explained.

"Old man, you stay where you are if you know what's good for you," Bradley warned before he marched into the house and went directly to the kitchen. There he saw the table, shoved it aside, and removed a small rug to discover the trapdoor. He pulled the small iron latch and opened the door. It creaked loudly until it was opened fully. "C'mon out."

Gabriel peeked out from the shadows and said, "Hello."

"Get out of there, boy, c'mon," Bradley barked.

"I can't. Miss Abigail said I needed to stay in here," Gabriel said, a look of fear on his face.

"Come on out, boy, now!" Bradley barked.

Gabriel urinated on himself and began to tremble in fear. "Sorry, mister, I don't know you. My aunt says—"

"Gabriel, you get on out of there, you hear. Come now," Abigail hollered from the kitchen doorway, her eyes bloodshot from crying and her lips swollen from getting hit.

Hearing Abigail's voice, Gabriel crawled out and ran to her. The two embraced. Immediately, Abigail noticed he was wet. "Oh, my poor child, you wet yourself."

"I'm sorry, I…I got scared. The man is scary," Gabriel said, looking at Bradley over his shoulder.

"This boy ain't yours. Whose is he?" Bradley asked.

"He's mine, sure is. I've been watching him for years now ever since his mama died," Abigail said.

"But what about Aunt Helen?" Gabriel blurted out.

"Aunt Helen? Where's Aunt Helen?" Bradley asked, stepping towards the two.

"You leave the boy alone, you hear me?" Abigail said, shoving Gabriel behind her and standing defiantly in between him and Bradley.

"You lied. I don't like when people lie to me," Bradley said.

A shrieking creak sounded behind Bradley. He turned to see Daniel coming through the rear door off the back porch. In his hands he held an 1860 Army Colt. "Die, you son of a bitch!" he hollered, pulling the trigger. The hammer on the pistol fell, striking the percussion cap. A second later the .44-caliber round ball exploded from the barrel, whizzed by Bradley's head, and impacted into the far wall. Needing to use both hands, Daniel held the pistol and cocked it.

Taking advantage of Daniel's slow speed, Bradley quickly drew his Schofield, cocked and fired. The .45-caliber round blasted out of the muzzle and struck Daniel squarely in the chest.

The force of the gunshot caused Daniel to drop his pistol and lurch forward.

Bradley wasn't one to give anyone a second chance. He cocked and fired two more times in quick succession, both shots accurately and lethally striking Daniel, who toppled to the floor dead. "I warned you, old man."

With Bradley focused on Daniel, Abigail saw an opportunity and struck out. She grabbed a heavy ceramic vase from the sideboard and slammed it against Bradley's head.

Bradley grunted and stumbled forward, but the blow wasn't enough to knock him out. He shook it off, pivoted, cocked the pistol, and pulled the trigger. Like before, the .45-caliber Smith & Wesson round proved effective, striking Abigail in the lower abdomen.

She bent over in pain and dropped to her knees.

Gabriel wailed in terror at the sight and ran towards her. "Miss Abigail."

Showing he didn't discriminate, Bradley stood upright, cocked the pistol, aimed it at her head, and said, "Look at me."

She lifted her head and spat, "To hell with you, evil white folk."

"You got spirit. I like that," Bradley said and squeezed the trigger.

## MILLS FARM, ST. JOSEPH, MISSOURI

Helen and John rode at a full gallop until they reached the spot. She jumped from the saddle, pulled a small entrenching tool from the saddlebag, and marched towards the base of the lone oak tree that sat atop the hill.

John dismounted and said, "You packed a shovel?"

"I came prepared," she said just before driving the small-headed shovel into the ground.

Not one to let a woman work while he stood idly by, he stepped up behind her, reached down and touched the shovel. "Please, let me do it."

She gave him a stern look and said, "I'm more than

capable."

"I know you are, but I can probably wield that shovel faster," he said in a gentle tone.

She tossed a scoop of earth and went for another. "If I get tired, then you can take over."

He stood up and said, "Fine."

She gave him a wink and said, "Thank you for reminding me that chivalry isn't dead."

He nodded and gave her a smile.

Displaying her grit and strength, Helen dug until the blade of the shovel struck something hard. She bent down and swept away the dirt to expose the metal lid of a foot-long rectangular chest. "There it is," she said, feeling relieved. She dug around and loosened the dirt that surrounded it, making it easier to pull out. Wiping her sweaty brow with her forearm, she gave John a look and said, "Now I'll need those muscles."

"Thought you'd never ask," he said, stepping forward. He reached down, took hold of a side and lifted, but found the box too heavy to pull out with one arm.

Seeing his trouble, she said, "I buried that by myself."

Struggling to get his other hand on the opposite handle, he chuckled. "You did? Remind me not to arm wrestle you."

"You're the only person who's seen this, I mean, outside of the others; no one knows this was here."

He heaved and brought the box out of the hole, his veins popping out of his neck. With a thud he dropped it on the ground, the contents' clanging revealing to his ears the chest was full of coins.

With the chest sitting in front of her, she merely stared at it.

After a pause he asked, "Well, now what?"

"I buried that twelve years ago. Hard to believe so much time has passed. This was my husband's legacy; inside that box is what he left me. I'd give it all back to have him here with me, to have had him all these years."

"Sorry," he said.

"Such a waste and for what?" she said, referencing the wastefulness the war had wrought on her.

He'd uttered those same words about the war before. He knew exactly where she was coming from, especially for those like them who fought so hard only to have their homes ravaged and their loved ones killed.

A silence fell over them for an untold time period, both reflecting on their lives before.

"I can't explain why, but I trust you. Please tell me I'm doing the right thing," she said, breaking the quiet between them.

His stomach tightened because his feelings for her were truthful, but the only reason he'd met her was due to a lie. "You can trust me. I wouldn't harm you."

"What is it about you? The second I met you, I felt like I'd known you for a long time. Is that odd?"

"I felt the same way," John replied.

She smiled and extended her arm until her hand touched his face. "Thank you, John."

"You're welcome."

Her eyes melted into his, and before he could think

about not doing it, he leaned over and kissed her on the lips.

With anyone else she would have recoiled, but not him. She welcomed the kiss and returned it with one more passionate. The two embraced briefly before she pulled away. "Let's get back."

"Sure," he said, pulling back. He looked at the box and asked, "Shall we open it up?"

"No need. That will pay what I owe him plus a bit more that I'll need to get me and Gabriel out of here," she said.

Shocked, he asked, "You're leaving?"

"Yes, I thought about it. I've had a good run here, turned this farm around, and made it successful. However, this situation with the bounty hunter only reminds me of the troubled past I lived. I don't want any part of it anymore. If Gabriel is going to live a peaceful life, I need to start fresh somewhere."

"Kentucky?" he asked.

"Maybe, I even thought about Georgia. I hear it's beautiful there," she quipped.

He smiled and said, "It's God's country."

"It's not that I don't believe in what we fought for during the war, or that my helping those afterwards was wrong. I don't, I have no regrets, but I never imagined I'd have to deal with those consequences years later," she confessed.

Cueing in on her few select words, he asked, "Helping those afterwards?"

"Although the war officially ended for many after

Johnston and Lee surrendered, it didn't here; it raged on through sixty-six," she explained, referencing the guerilla war fought by Confederate partisans against the Missouri state government, which was finally squashed in December of 1866. The remaining members of that resistance—Frank and Jesse James as well as Cole Younger—went on to form the James-Younger Gang.

John understood how allegiances had been strained during the tumultuous ending of the war, with many wanting to return to peace while others wanted to continue the fight. He was curious, though, who she was referring to. He assumed it was the same people who shared in the spoils of the stolen gold.

As they secured the chest to his horse, he couldn't resist but ask the question that was burning in his mind. "Helen?"

"Yes."

"What kind of support did you give after the war?"

"Shelter, food mainly," she answered as she tightened the saddle on her horse.

He mounted his horse and asked, "Can I ask a personal question?"

"Sure."

He thought about how he'd phrase the question without it sounding odd but couldn't, so he asked it bluntly. "Did any of those people you helped after the war happen to be Frank or Jesse James?"

She looked away, not wanting to answer, but not before he caught an uncomfortable expression on her face.

"Are you okay?" he asked.

"Yes, I'm fine; just that I haven't spoken their names in so long," she said, petting the mane of her horse.

"I don't mean to pry," he lied.

"No, it's fine and, yes, I helped them; I provided them support during and after the war. We parted ways in the spring of sixty-seven. I needed to get the farm working and couldn't be distracted by helping outlaws. They said they were continuing the fight, but really they'd become nothing but ruthless marauders," she said, staring off into the distance. A strong wind slammed into her, almost blowing the hat off her head. She readjusted it and continued, "Why do you ask about them? It's a random thing to query."

"They're famous is all. I've read about them in the papers, and I heard they were from these parts, so I just wondered."

She nodded.

"What's your take on what happened to them in Minnesota?" he asked.

"I don't have a take. Those who choose to live by the gun often die by it," she said.

Her last comment struck him. He had for many years and was still living by the gun; was his fate written for him? Would he perish like the many he'd killed?

She mounted her horse and gave him a look. "What are you thinking?"

"Just what you said, about living and dying by the gun," he replied. He had one last question to ask and knew there was no good way to say it, so he just blurted it out. "Do you know where they are?"

"Who?" she asked, pretending not to know whom he was talking about.

"The James brothers. A lot of people are looking for them, and I thought you might know since you were close with them."

She pulled her horse alongside him and answered directly, "I said I haven't seen them since sixty-seven. Why so curious about the James brothers?"

"Like I said, they're famous."

"More like infamous. I don't have anything to do with them or their criminality."

"I see my questions struck a nerve, I apologize. I wasn't implying you were involved with them," John said.

"A lot of questions for a farmhand," she quipped.

"I'm a big reader of dime novels is all," he replied.

She gave him a weary look and said, "Come on, dime novel reader, let's get this gold to Daniel and figure out *our* next step." She kicked the sides of her horse and took off at a full gallop.

"Our?" he asked himself, liking the sound of the word.

\*\*\*

The ride back to Daniel's house was uneventful until they saw the plume of smoke rising above the hill.

With urgency, Helen sprinted away, leaving John trotting along with the chest strapped to the back of his horse.

"Helen, wait!" John called out, watching her pull away fast. Not wanting to ride into a situation with a chest full of gold, John pulled out his knife and cut the straps holding the chest. It fell off the back of his horse and slammed into the ground with a loud thud. Free of the bulky and heavy chest, he bolted after her. When he cleared the hill and looked down, he saw the source of the smoke was a fire inside the house.

"Gabriel!" Helen cried out as she dismounted the horse and ran up to the back of the house.

"Wait!" John hollered. "Don't go inside. Wait!"

Helen grabbed the doorknob but quickly recoiled, as it was searing hot. "Gabriel!"

John reached the house, jumped from the horse, and ran up to Helen. He peered in through the back window and saw the fire had engulfed the kitchen. "We need to try to go in from the front," John said, leaving her side and running around to the front.

All Helen could think about was Gabriel. Where was he? Was he still alive? Was he in the house?

John reached the front and found a grisly sight. Leaning up against the side of the house was Abigail. It was evident she was dead by the gaping hole in the back of her head. On her chest he saw a blood-soaked note; it was held in place by a knife. John clenched his jaw in anger. There was no doubt who had done this. He was approaching Abigail's body when a loud shriek sounded from behind him; it was Helen.

She had made it around to the front and saw Abigail's body. "Oh no, no!"

John's instincts were to run inside to find Gabriel, but the note drew him in because clearly visible at the bottom, written large and bold, was the name GABRIEL.

"Gabriel!" Helen screamed and ran for the open front door.

John pulled the note off Abigail's chest and read it. *'WANT THE BOY? COME TO THE OLD MILL.'* Below that inscription was another note clearly written by Gabriel. It read *'SAVE ME, GABRIEL.'*

"Gabriel!" Helen continued to scream. She ran onto the porch and was about to enter the smoke-filled house when John stopped her.

"He's not in there," John said, handing her the note.

Holding the note in her trembling hands, she read it. With tears streaming down her face, she wailed. "Oh my boy, my sweet boy."

John put his arms around her and said, "I'll get him back, I will, I swear it."

"What have I done?" she asked, embracing John tightly.

The sounds of heavy galloping sounded behind them. John turned to see three men riding up fast. He squinted and recognized it was Graham. "It's the sheriff."

Helen folded the note and shoved it into a pocket of her skirt.

Graham rode up and dismounted before stopping his horse. "Helen, are you okay?"

"He has Gabriel. He has my boy," she said.

Fowler and Lee trotted up but remained in their saddles.

Graham put his hands on her shoulders in an effort to comfort her and said, "I'll do everything in my power to find him."

Helen wiped the flowing tears from her face and simply nodded.

"Do you have any idea where he might have taken him?"

Helen nodded but didn't reply.

"Where?" Graham asked.

Bringing his experience to bear, John said, "First, let's step away from this house, and second, we can't be going in guns blazing, we need a plan. Frank Bradley is a force to reckon with, and if we're going to get Gabriel back alive, we need to think this through."

"Who's we? I'm the sheriff. My deputies and I will be handling this," Graham snapped.

"Graham, if John wants to help, let him, and just know that I'm going as well," Helen said.

Graham went to protest, but Helen interrupted him. "If you want to help me get Gabriel back, I'll be involved, period."

"Very well," Graham said with a nod.

## MILLS FARM, ST. JOSEPH, MISSOURI

With Daniel's house destroyed, the group went to Helen's house to formulate a strategy and plan. The entire ride over, Graham kept his eye on John. He could see how Helen looked at him and wondered if the two had become something more. Not wanting to derail Helen's need for him; he decided to lie low and show her how valuable he could be.

Helen wasn't upset nor fazed by the condition of her house. She'd heard it had been torn apart, but sometime in between her leaving for Daniel's and now, she'd divorced herself of caring for the property. She immediately went to the dining room and cleared the table.

The men followed her inside and stood watching her, each carefully and anxiously eyeing the other.

"I'd ask if you need something to drink, but you know where the kitchen is," Helen said, taking a seat.

"I could use some water," Fowler said, exiting the room.

"Get some for all of us," Graham hollered. He turned to face Helen and asked, "You suggested that you know where Gabriel might be. Is that true?"

"Yes," Helen said.

"And where might that be?" Graham asked.

"The old mill off the Sutter creek," Helen replied.

"Can I ask how you know that?" Graham asked.

"He left a note, said he was there," Helen answered.

"Anyone know that mill? How it's laid out?" Graham asked, looking around the room.

Overhearing from the kitchen, Fowler cried out, "I do. I used to play there when I was young. I know the place like the back of my hand."

"Get in here and draw us a layout and map of the area," Graham ordered.

Fowler entered the room holding a tray; on it was a

pitcher of water and five glasses. He set it on the table and said, "Right away, Sheriff."

While Fowler went to work on the map, Graham had other questions. "Helen, what does he want?"

She looked down, not wanting to answer fully.

"And please don't say you don't know. A man like Frank Bradley doesn't kidnap your nephew unless you have something he wants. He's here for a reason," Graham said, knowing she was holding out critical information.

"Can I speak with you in private?" Helen asked Graham.

Seeing an opportunity to get close and regain trust with her, he replied, "Of course."

The two exited the room and went outside. She led him to the end of the porch, turned and said, "He thinks I know where Frank and Jesse James might be hiding."

Shocked by her comment, he asked, "Do you?"

"Of course not, but do I tell him that?" she asked, unsure how to proceed.

Graham rubbed his chin and thought. "He's come a long way and seems to think you know; why would he think you would?"

"Can we stick to thinking about how I'll deal with this?" Helen asked.

"Just answer the question, Helen; why would he think you know?" Graham insisted.

"Because I helped them out many years ago, just after the war. Somehow he feels my helping them then equals my knowing about their whereabouts now," she answered, only telling half the truth. She didn't want to divulge the part of the story concerning the gold.

"I knew your husband fought alongside them during the war. I wasn't aware you helped them afterwards," Graham said, acting shocked at the revelation.

"You and I both know how complicated things were after the war. Let's not debate that time period; it was tough enough living through it," she snapped.

Agreeing, he moved on from the point. "I think you go there prepared to tell him what you know. What we should do is draw him out. When he's in the open, we can take him down."

"Okay," she said. "And, Graham, please share with no one what I told you about my affiliation with the James brothers. It was a lifetime ago; I'm not the same person."

He patted his chest with his open hand and said, "Your secret stays with me."

The two came back inside.

John was dying to know what she had divulged to Graham but would wait to find out when the timing was appropriate. He looked at Fowler and asked, "Are you done yet?"

"One more minute," Fowler replied, feverishly sketching on a large piece of paper.

Lee, who sat silent, watching the back and forth, raised his hand.

"This isn't school. Speak your mind," Graham said, acknowledging Lee.

"Does anyone have any plan at all?" Lee asked the

group.

Wanting to appear in charge, Graham answered the question. "Me and Helen will ride to the mill to meet Bradley. The rest of you will set up in positions farther out, armed with rifles."

"I want John with me," she said, interrupting Graham.

"I'm the sheriff. I should go with you," Graham insisted.

"No, John goes with me," she said.

Graham stewed, shooting John a wary gaze.

"How do you know he'll abide by the terms of the trade?" Lee asked.

"You said he visited McKinney, right?" Helen asked.

"Yes," Graham answered.

"McKinney is still alive. I can only assume he gave him what he wanted," Helen said.

"But what was that?" Lee asked.

"That's not important. What's important is getting Gabriel back," Graham said.

Lee nodded, satisfied with the answer.

"Done!" Fowler exclaimed, slapping the sketch in the middle of the table. He pointed at the paper and began to describe what was drawn. "In the middle is the old mill. There's an entrance here and there, only two; there's also a door in the floor that the workers used to access the race, which runs in both directions here and here. The mill is surrounded on three sides by a slight grade where one or two of us could cover it. Across the creek is the old Hemet house. Nothing is left but a foundation, but someone in those old ruins could get a clear view of the entire creek and the old mill in the event Bradley heads that way."

"That's it. I go in with John just behind me. You three cover the area from those places the deputy just mentioned," Helen said.

"I don't like it. I think I should go with you. John here isn't equipped to protect you," Graham said.

"Trust me, Sheriff, I'm more than capable of handling myself and protecting Helen," John said confidently.

"You're a damn field hand—"

"A field hand who used to be a deputy sheriff in Tucson," John blurted out, immediately regretting the information he just divulged.

Helen cocked her head and asked, "You were a deputy sheriff in Tucson?"

"It's in the past. Let's get back to the plan," John said, wanting to move on.

Graham leaned back in his seat and gave John a curious look.

John met his gaze and knew he was questioning just who he was.

"John's right. Let's get back to the plan. We can't waste any more time; Gabriel needs me," Helen said.

"Fine, I'll take the old Hemet house. Lee, you take a position on the east ridge, and Fowler on the west ridge. If you get a clear shot at him, take it," Graham ordered.

"But only after I have Gabriel. Does everyone understand?" Helen said, looking at each man.

Everyone nodded.

"Good, let's go get Gabriel," Helen said.

Everyone stood and began to exit. Helen approached Graham and pulled him aside. "I want to thank you—"

Interrupting her, he replied, "No need. I'm here because it's my job but more importantly because I care about you."

She touched his arm out of a genuine appreciation and continued, "But it should be said, and I mean it. Thank you. Had you not warned me, things could have been worse."

"I've told you for a long time that I'm here for you. I only wish you'd give me a chance," he said.

Seeing he was going there once more, she put the brakes on it. "I know, and you know how I feel. Let's stay focused on getting Gabriel back."

"Fair enough."

She rubbed his arm and smiled.

John brushed by on his way out the door.

Graham gave him a look then turned to Helen and said, "You don't know that man. Why are you putting so much trust in him?"

Her smile widened, her gaze now fixed on John. "Because I do know him; I feel I've known him my whole life. I know it sounds odd, but I do."

Sensing she was falling in love with John, Graham grew agitated. "You didn't know he was a deputy sheriff. Helen, don't be naïve. He only arrived in town recently."

"You're right, I don't know everything about him, but I feel like I *know* him. I understand it sounds silly," she answered. "Graham, none of this helps Gabriel. Let's stay focused and go get him."

"Agreed, let's bring him back," Graham said, catching sight of John. He clenched his jaw tightly and asked himself, *Who is this John Nance?* He wasn't sure, but he now had a clue to find out.

## OLD MILL, ST. JOSEPH, MISSOURI

John could see the tension written all over Helen's face. Every few seconds she'd lift her head and look in the direction of the mill, expecting to see Gabriel or even Bradley coming their way. It was enough for him to speak up. "We'll get him back. I hope you believe that."

She faced him and replied, "I believe it, but I still can't help but be nervous at the same time. I just know he's terrified, and I can't be there to comfort him. What he must be going through, it just makes my stomach turn."

"Gabriel strikes me as a tough kid, a sweet one, nice, but tough; I'd give him more credit," John said, hoping that would ease her fears.

"He is resilient, but this, seeing what happened to Abigail, that must have been truly terrifying," she said, looking towards the horses when she heard one neigh. Spotting the chest, she continued, "Thank you for riding all the way back and getting the chest. At first I was annoyed that you had to go back, but it did make sense. You didn't want to bring it down to the house."

"I didn't know what we were riding into," John

explained.

"No, I understand. I'm just so anxious; I want this entire ordeal to be over," she said, clenching and squeezing her hands.

He placed his hand on top of hers gingerly and said, "Have you thought more about leaving Missouri?"

"On the ride back to the house and here, I did. What closed the deal was seeing my past come back in such a way it killed poor Abigail and terrorized Gabriel. There's no guarantee something like this won't happen again. When I aligned myself after the war with the James and Younger brothers, I made a mistake. I set into motion everything that happened today," she said.

"If you need my help, I'm at your service," John said, hoping and praying she'd say yes.

"What time is it?" she asked.

He pulled out a gold pocket watch, flipped it open, and said, "One more minute. Let's saddle up."

They got on their horses and began the slow ride to the mill.

As they closed in, John scanned the area for anything peculiar, but saw nothing. Tied up out front was a single horse. No doubt it belonged to Bradley. When the two were thirty feet away, Bradley stepped into the open entryway with a pistol in his right hand and a clearly tormented Gabriel in his left.

Helen's stomach tightened, and a sensation of nausea struck her upon seeing Gabriel. She wanted nothing more at that moment than to ride up and shoot Bradley between the eyes.

"That's close enough!" Bradley shouted.

The two came to a full stop.

"I don't know who you are but carefully pull any weapons you have and toss them on the ground. Do it, do it now!" Bradley hollered. He pressed the muzzle firmly into Gabriel's temple.

"Do what he says," Helen ordered John.

Without question or hesitation, John pulled his Colt from his holster and tore the Winchester from its scabbard and tossed them both on the ground.

"You too, little lady, I know you're carrying," Bradley snorted.

Not wanting to jeopardize the transaction, Helen removed the Colt she had buried in her skirt pocket and threw it to the ground. "I have the information you want."

"Good. Now dismount and come towards me. We need to chat," Bradley ordered.

Helen did as he said and came to him.

"Stop right there," Bradley ordered when she was a few feet away. He gave her a once-over then asked, "Where are the James brothers?"

"I don't know."

Bradley pressed the muzzle of the barrel into Gabriel's temple, causing him to cry, and Bradley barked, "Tell me the truth, or I put a round through these mushy brains."

Knowing he wouldn't believe that answer, she lied, "They're in Nashville, just north of the city. Where exactly, I'm not sure."

"Are you lying?" Bradley asked.

"That's the last I heard concerning their whereabouts. Now let Gabriel go," Helen said.

"Give me more details about Nashville," Bradley said.

"Their mother, Zerelda, moved there recently. I heard the brothers followed," Helen said.

Bradley looked deeply into her eyes and remained quiet. After a minute of silence he spoke. "The gold you helped steal. Do you still have it? Any of it?"

"No, spent it years ago," Helen again lied.

"Your friend, tell him to advance," Bradley said.

"Why?" Helen asked.

"Just do it," Bradley exclaimed, pressing the muzzle into Gabriel's temple again, this time harder, making him yelp.

"Don't hurt him!" she hollered.

"Then listen to me," Bradley barked.

Helen turned and waved for John to advance.

John did exactly what she said. As he moved farther away from his weapons, he grew uneasy.

"Stop right there," Bradley ordered when John was just behind Helen. "Dismount and step away from the horse, far away."

John did everything he was asked although he contemplated pulling his knife and lunging at Bradley but refrained from acting because the risk was too high for Gabriel and Helen.

"How did you find out about me?"

"I have my ways of finding out information."

Bradley chuckled.

"How?" Helen asked. "Humor me."

"It doesn't matter," Bradley said.

"It does to me," Helen said.

"Listen here, little lady, I don't have time for your stupid questions. Now go join your friend," Bradley barked.

"I'm not leaving without Gabriel," Helen said defiantly.

"You'll get him when I'm safely away," Bradley said.

"No, that wasn't part of the deal. I give you information, you give me Gabriel, that was the deal," Helen snapped.

"Do you honestly think I don't know there are men on those hills and across the creek? You must really think I'm stupid." Bradley chuckled. "I have eyes in the back of my head and hearing as good as any critter."

"You won't leave with him. I won't allow it," Helen said, stepping towards him.

Bradley raised his pistol and leveled it at her face. "Step back."

"Take me instead. If you need insurance, take me until you feel safely away," Helen demanded.

Hearing her, John shouted, "Helen, no, don't do that."

"You shut up back there," Bradley yelled. He thought about the offer and said, "Fine, you're prettier, and I bet you haven't crapped your pants."

Helen stepped forward until she was in arm's reach.

Bradley shoved Gabriel out of the way and snatched

Helen by the neck. He pulled her close and sniffed. "You do smell better."

John began to advance. "Helen, don't do this."

Bradley aimed his pistol at John and said, "If your friend wants to die, all he needs to do is keep coming."

Helen turned and hollered, "John, stay where you are. I'll be fine. Take care of Gabriel."

John stopped his advance, his fists clenched in anger.

Standing up, Gabriel comprehended what was happening and wailed, "Aunt Helen, don't go with him. He's a bad man, a very bad man. He killed Abigail, shot her in the head."

"Sweetheart, I'll be fine. You're safe now. Look to my friend John. He'll take care of you until I return," Helen said, pointing towards John.

"Get on the horse," Bradley ordered.

Helen mounted the horse, her focus still on Gabriel. A calmness enveloped her, as she knew Gabriel was now safe.

"No, Aunt Helen, don't go. He'll hurt you, please."

Bradley swung himself on top of the horse and laughed loudly. "All you bastards out there hiding, if you do one thing, I'll put a bullet in her pretty little head!"

Watching in shock from across the creek, Graham didn't know what to do. Now more than any time in his life he wanted to fight but knew any action he took could get Helen killed. Feeling helpless, he remained hidden behind the old foundation.

Tears burst from Gabriel's eyes, and his cries turned to wailing. "No, Aunt Helen, don't go with him, don't!"

"I'll be fine, I promise," Helen said.

Gabriel lowered his head and sobbed loudly. On the ground a foot from him was a large rock about the size of a man's fist. Suddenly, without thinking, he bent down, picked it up, and held it in his hand.

Seeing him, Helen called out, "Gabriel, don't do anything, please."

Bradley was adjusting himself in the saddle and stopped to look at what Helen was talking about, to see Gabriel standing with his right arm raised. In his grip was a rock. "Boy, don't be stupid."

"You let my aunt Helen go!" Gabriel screamed, tears streaming down his face and spit flying as he spoke.

"Well, I have to give it to him, the boy does have a pair of balls. I thought he was a bit mushy in the head, but he does seem to have some grit." Bradly chuckled in his deep raspy voice. Unconcerned about Gabriel, Bradley took the reins and steered the horse towards the creek.

"No!" Gabriel screamed. He ran at Bradley and threw the rock as hard as he could. In a one-in-a-million shot, the rock connected perfectly with the back of Bradley's head.

Bradley dropped the reins and bobbed back and forth in the saddle.

Seeing an opportunity, John sprinted towards a dazed Bradley.

Also taking advantage, Helen swung back with her elbow and hit Bradley in the jaw.

This blow was enough to topple him off the horse. His massive body hit the ground with a loud thud.

Bradley grunted and attempted to roll onto his side, but John was too fast and reached him before he could make the transition.

John straddled his torso and began to pummel him with punches, one after another.

Looking on, Gabriel watched in awe as John pounded away on Bradley.

After witnessing the altercation from the safety of the foundation, Graham knew he had to get involved. He sprang from the spot and sprinted across the knee-deep creek with his Winchester rifle in hand.

John wasn't letting up; he kept hammering away at Bradley. He'd met men like him, and if he let up too soon, Bradley would come back with a vengeance. The delicate balance was not killing him. He wanted to know who sent him and needed answers that only he could give.

Graham arrived, gave John a quick glance, then went to Helen, who was still in the saddle, watching as if in a trance the beating John was leveling on Bradley. "Are you okay?"

"I'm fine," she answered, not tearing her gaze from John.

"That's enough. Don't kill him," Graham barked. "I want to interrogate him."

"Kill him, John, kill the son of a bitch!" Helen barked. Her desire for Bradley's demise was twofold. She wanted him dead out of revenge for what he had done to Gabriel and Abigail, and she didn't want him talking. She wasn't sure what else he might know that he could divulge to Graham, further eroding her position.

Bradley's face was a bloody and battered mess. The flesh from his nose was torn away and smeared across his left cheek, his eyes were swollen shut, and several deep cuts on his cheeks were gushing blood.

John hesitated to catch his breath; beating someone senseless was a tiring affair. He looked at his right hand. It was sore but not broken. He'd heard Helen's plea and planned on doing as she instructed. After taking another deep breath, he began to pound away on Bradley's face.

"Stop, that's enough. I want the man for questioning," Graham yelled, coming up behind John and pulling him off.

Angered by Graham's response and willing to suffer the consequences, Helen jumped from the horse, picked up the rock Gabriel had thrown initially, held it in her hand, and began to slam it against Bradley's face.

Shocked that Helen was now beating the unconscious Bradley, Graham cried out, "What are you doing? If you kill him, that'll be murder."

She stopped, looked at Graham and laughed. "Really? You'd arrest me for murdering this devil, this evil man? No, Graham, this is justice." She held the rock high above her head and brought it down with all of her might against his face. The sound of his facial bones crushing sounded like a musical note to her ears. "That was for Abigail, you son of a bitch!" Sensing he was dead, she tossed the bloody rock aside, got to her feet, and walked over to a gawking Graham. "You don't give evil a trial, you destroy it."

"But he could have told us some critical information," Graham countered.

Ignoring him, Helen walked over to Gabriel and embraced him tightly. "How's my boy?"

"You killed the bad man?" he asked, his head buried in her shoulder.

"I think I did," she replied.

Fowler and Lee appeared from opposite directions.

"Holy smokes, in all my days, I've never seen a woman act so...brutal," Lee said with a broad smile stretched across his face, clearly finding joy in viewing Helen's wrath.

"Then you haven't met my mother," Fowler joked.

Neither man seemed concerned about what they'd witnessed. Graham alone stood in opposition.

John stepped up behind Helen and Gabriel. He placed his hand tenderly on her shoulder. "How's he doing?"

She looked up at him and replied, "I think he'll be fine. I just need to get him home, cleaned up, and put a hot meal in his belly," she said, caressing Gabriel's back.

"You beat the man real good," Gabriel exclaimed to John.

"I did what anyone would do. I promised your mother I'd do whatever it took to get you back safely," John said.

"She's my aunt Helen, but she's like my mother. My real mother died—" Gabriel said. He was getting ready to repeat the same story about his mother dying, but John interrupted him.

"She's your mother, Gabriel. Believe me, she's your mother," John said, pointing at Helen.

"What will the judge say about this?" Graham asked, his body language signaling to everyone he was miffed.

Helen and John ignored him. Instead she reached up and drew John in close and kissed him. "Thank you."

"Anytime," John said after the kiss.

The public display of affection between Helen and John sent Graham's blood boiling. Not wanting to lose his wits, he walked off.

"Now what?" John asked.

"Like I said, we take him home. Tomorrow we start picking up the pieces, starting with Abigail. We'll bring her home and bury her proper," Helen said.

"Fair enough."

Graham remained at the old mill with his deputies. As he watched Helen, John and Gabriel ride off, his temper flared. He'd put aside his revenge against her when he thought he had an opportunity to win her over, but seeing them together told him he'd never have her, and if he couldn't, he'd do whatever he could to ensure no one could.

# CHAPTER SIX

"Truths and roses have thorns about them." – Henry
David Thoreau

## ST. JOSEPH, MISSOURI

## NOVEMBER 13, 1876

After a consultation with the judge and his two deputies, Graham decided not to pursue murder charges against Helen even though he was tempted to defy them all and arrest her. The rage he'd felt that day after witnessing her and John's intimacy was still boiling inside him, and he desperately wanted to strike out at both of them. Upon returning to his office on that fateful day, he'd immediately made inquiries to the local authorities in Tucson concerning John; he needed to know who he was and if his story checked out.

The killing of Frank Bradley was heralded as a success for the sheriff's office, with his deputies reveling in the praise. Graham was too focused on how he could topple Helen and John.

An impatient man, the waiting for information ate at Graham and drove him to drink. In the following days, he could be found at the Great Ox every night, and his once sober reputation was being destroyed with each passing evening.

Then a knock came on his door. It was a knock he'd

been expecting, and the person behind the door was about to give him something he could use against Helen.

Hungover, he staggered to the door and unlocked it. "Who the hell is knocking at seven thirty?" He swung the door wide and looked out to find Evan, the postal manager. "Evan, what the hell are you doing at my house?"

"Received a package for you, Sheriff," Evan answered, his expression showing the shock he was feeling seeing Graham in a disheveled state.

"This couldn't wait 'til later?" Graham growled.

"Sheriff, you specifically asked me to personally deliver any packages to your house if they came in early or late. Don't you remember?" Evan said, defending the early morning special delivery.

Graham scratched his head as he searched for that memory. Finding it, he said, "Yeah, yeah, I remember. Here, give it to me." He took the small parcel that was wrapped in thick brown paper. Not concerned with Evan any longer, he turned and slammed the door in his face. As he walked towards his kitchen, he found the return address and noticed it was from Samuel Chase. "Yes!" he exclaimed as he ripped the wrapping off to reveal a thick ledger inside. Being ever efficient, Samuel had bookmarked the pages for quick reference. Graham turned to the first bookmark and ran his finger from the top of the page down until he saw what he was looking for. There in black ink was written *HELEN SUE MILLS, TAX DEFERMENT, JULY 23, 1865*, and next to the date was her signature. For each year, Samuel had her name listed. The timeline on his ledger ended when he retired. "You old codger, keeping your own personal ledger, how brilliant."

Then he remembered the gold she had; it was clearly enough to pay the back taxes. All he'd do was cause her an inconvenience. He tossed the ledger on the table and headed to his bedroom to get ready for the day. As he washed, another knock came to his door. He peeked out from his bedroom and called out, "Whoever it is, come in!"

The door creaked open. "Hello."

Toweling off his face, he replied, "Who is it?"

"Sheriff, I have an urgent telegram!" the Western Union clerk cried out. He looked around the house and was disturbed by how untidy it was. On the dining table were rows of empty bottles, and plates covered with old food were stacked in the middle. Dirty clothes were strewn all over the floor, and a moldy stale odor filled the room.

Hearing that he had an urgent telegram, he rushed from the bedroom wearing only trousers. He marched up and snatched the paper from the clerk's hand. He quickly unfolded it and read *JOHN NANCE WAS NOT A DEPUTY SHERIFF. HOWEVER, A JOHN SMITH WAS A DEPUTY SHERIFF IN TUCSON. LEFT IN AUGUST. WHEREABOUTS UNKNOWN. – SHERIFF WHEELER.* Graham thought about the telegram, wondering if John Nance was John Smith. If it was, why did he change his name, or had he been under an alias while working as a deputy sheriff? None of this was enough to cause a controversy. Once again, feeling let down, he folded the note and tossed it on the side table.

"Any reply?" the clerk asked.

"No," Graham answered, disappointment sounding in his tone.

"Something wrong, Sheriff?"

Normally not one to openly complain to someone like the Western Union clerk, he said, "A lot is wrong. Life in general is wrong. I'm trying to get information on someone in town, to…help with an investigation. I was expecting this telegram would help, but all it's done is add more confusion."

The clerk opened his mouth to speak but hesitated.

Seeing this, Graham asked, "What is it?"

"Thing is I might have some information about John Nance, but I'm sworn to confidentiality. If Western Union were to find out, I could lose my job," the clerk said.

Graham grabbed the clerk by the shoulder, pulled him into the house and slammed the door. "What do you know?"

"I don't want to lose my job," the clerk said sheepishly.

"You won't, I swear," Graham said.

"I don't know," the clerk said, now regretting his offer to give information.

"Nothing will happen to you. Tell me what you know," Graham snapped, veins in his neck throbbing.

"Mr. Nance sends and receives telegrams every few

days to the North Nashville office. Sends them to a man named Garrett Vane. This Garrett Vane was in town about a week ago. I believe he arrived at the beginning of the month. I recollect it was November 3; yes, that was it. He said he'd just arrived on the train and was staying for a while. We chatted…"

"About what? Hurry up, spit out something crucial," Graham barked.

"Um, sorry, we chatted about nothing, really, the weather, and, um, the messages that Mr. Nance receives are about that…the weather."

"What does that mean, the weather?" Graham asked, confused.

"He receives one-word telegrams, a couple of them. In fact, I have one back at the office now. They simply say cloudy."

"Cloudy? What in the hell does that mean?"

"And what's even more peculiar is Mr. Nance replies to the telegram with the same word…cloudy."

Graham thought for a moment; then it hit him. "That's it, it's a code. Cloudy isn't the weather, it's a code for something."

The clerk stood speechless and rigid; his regret for opening up now turned to fear. It was apparent Graham was erratic and possibly not trustworthy.

"Anything else? Think, think," Graham barked.

"There was a telegram that Garrett Vane received from someone in Chicago."

"Do you know what Western Union office it came from?" Graham asked.

"I don't recall," the clerk replied with trepidation in his voice.

"Think!" Graham snapped.

"I, um, I can't remember, sir, I'm sorry," the clerk replied, his voice cracking.

"Any other messages from Chicago?" Graham asked.

"No. That I know for sure," the clerk answered.

"How does this Garrett spell his last name?"

"V-A-N-E," the clerk replied.

Graham turned and began to pace his front room.

"Sir, will that be it? I really need to go back to the office."

Graham got an idea and ran to a small rolltop desk against the far wall. Taking a pencil and a blank piece of paper, he wrote a note, then folded the paper up and placed it in an envelope. He took the telegram from the Tucson sheriff and included it but added a handwritten note to it and slid it also into the envelope. He walked over to the clerk and handed it to him. "I need you to do something for me; it's urgent. Go back to your office, get that telegram for Mr. Nance, and place it in the envelope, then seal it. I then need you to ride out to the Mills Farm and deliver it to Mrs. Mills directly."

"Sir, that will make me late…"

"I need you; the people of Buchanan County need you," Graham said, racing back to the desk and grabbing a handful of coins. He went back and handed the money to the clerk. "That's forty dollars, more than enough for your time."

Wide-eyed, the clerk looked at the money. Now sold

on the task, he asked, "Anything else?"

Graham thought and suddenly had another idea that could disrupt whatever John might be up to with Garrett. "What's the opposite of cloudy?"

"Sunny?"

"Exactly!" Graham exclaimed. "Send a telegram to Garrett Vane with the one-word message SUNNY."

"Yes, sir," the clerk said, his anxiety gone, replaced with a sense of purpose.

"Now go, hurry, and don't utter a word to anyone about this," Graham said.

The clerk nodded and exited the house. He sprinted down the steps and towards the Western Union office.

Graham stepped onto his porch. He wasn't sure what he'd stumbled upon, but it could be something that could force a wedge in between Helen and John.

## MILLS FARM, ST. JOSEPH, MISSOURI

The days that followed the altercation with Frank Bradley could only be described as some of the best in John's life. Yes, there were tears when they laid Abigail to rest, and sleepless nights, as Gabriel often woke from nightmares because of his ordeal; but for John, who had lived so many years alone without the comfort of another, he now came to believe that he might have found love again.

It was such an unimaginable thing. How many times could one find true love? he asked himself. Yes, he'd loved Elizabeth when they'd met those many years ago, but theirs had been youthful infatuation and lust, which had resulted in Mary. His family was a blessing and he'd never take it back, nor would he ever long for a life without them, but what happened to them was out of his control. They'd been brutally murdered, and those murders led him on an exodus from his beloved lands in pursuit of revenge, only to find real closure came from forgiveness. That journey then led him to Dodge City, then on to Deadwood, and now here he was in St. Joseph, Missouri, holding the hand of a woman he never imagined could exist. Was it fate? Had God finally decided to bestow upon him the blessings of a woman and family? Whatever it was, he wasn't going to take it or her for granted. If God had given him a new lease on a normal and simple life, he'd take it; however, there was one thing that stood in the way, and it was the one thing that could destroy it all. He had to either abandon his pursuit of the James brothers or fulfill that mission; either way he had to come to grips with either telling her his real identity or not, with hopes she'd be understanding.

John entered the house to find Helen in the dining room, hovering over a table strewn with papers and documents. He could see she was stressed, but about what was unknown. "And I thought what I was doing was daunting," he joked.

"Trying to get everything organized. If I'm going to sell the farm and my other assets, I need to know exactly what I have," she said, taking several papers and stacking them on top of a pile to the left.

"So you are moving?" John asked.

She had mentioned leaving before, but they'd not

had a conversation where she formally declared her intentions until now.

"Yes, I told you, I can't risk having another incident happen. Just because we were able to stop Frank Bradley doesn't mean another won't come; in fact, I'm betting on it."

"Have you given any thought to coming to California with me?" he asked.

She looked up and replied, "I have, but how do I explain to Gabriel that we're leaving with a man he hardly knows?"

"I can make an honest woman out of you," he quipped, a large smile stretched across his face.

"Marriage?"

"Yes," he said, his tone shifting. Hearing that word come from his mouth made him pause.

"Tell me more about California," she said. "I need some convincing."

John walked farther into the room and took a seat. "There's a small town, if it's that, called Ojai. It's spelled O-J-A-I, but pronounced oh-high. They found oil there, and an article I read not long ago said that oil will have many commercial uses in the near future. One scholar called it black gold. Apparently it's so plentiful in the hills north of Los Angeles that it's seeping out of the ground. All you need to do is scoop it up."

"Sounds too good to be true," she said.

"Probably is, but it's far away from here and can provide us with a new opportunity that doesn't involve gambling, gold—"

"And the James brothers," she said, interrupting him.

"Exactly, and I hear the place is beautiful. Oh, and the Pacific Ocean is close by. I'll buy us a house right on it."

"Hmm, I've never seen the ocean, any ocean," she mused.

"Then come with me."

She looked at the stacks of documents and sighed. "I'll think about it. Let's talk later."

"Of course, I'm available when you need me," John said, taking his leave from the dining room. As he headed towards the front door, he saw a man walking up the front porch steps. "Aren't you the clerk from the Western Union office?"

"Yes, sir. I have an urgent message for Mrs. Mills," the clerk said, holding the envelope firmly in his grasp.

John opened the screen door and reached for the envelope. "Thank you."

The clerk recoiled and said, "No, sir, I'm to give this directly to Mrs. Mills."

"What?" John asked, finding the demand odd. He craned his head back and called out, "Helen, there's a telegram for you."

"Get it for me, please," she replied from the dining room.

"I can't. He's to deliver it to you personally," John said.

Helen walked up to the front door and stepped in front of John.

"Mrs. Mills?" the clerk asked.

"Yes."

"Urgent message," the clerk said and held out the envelope Graham had given him.

She took it and looked the envelope over but didn't see anything that told her what was inside.

The clerk loitered for a second, gave John a wary look, then headed off.

John couldn't imagine why he'd come all the way out here from town. He glanced at the envelope over Helen's shoulder and said, "That was strange."

"I wonder who it could be from?" she asked before tearing it open. She removed the three folded pieces of paper and gave John a puzzled look before unfolding the first one. As her eyes scanned the handwritten note, her brow furrowed. She opened the next one and had the same reaction.

Seeing her reaction, he asked, "Is there something wrong?"

"Who's John Smith? Is that you?" she asked.

Hearing the name he'd used in Tucson, he froze.

"I can see by the look on your face it is you," she said.

"Who's Garrett Vane?" she asked, looking up from the last page.

Needing to know what was written, John stepped forward and reached for the papers. "What do you have there?"

She recoiled and held them behind her back. "Who are you?"

He tried to reach around behind her back, but she

stepped away from him. "Just be honest with me. I need honesty."

"I used the name Smith when I was in Tucson a few months ago."

"Why?"

"I had my reasons."

"Tell me, is Nance your real last name?" she blurted out. Wanting space in between them, she slowly made her way around the table.

Frustrated because he didn't know who had sent the papers or what was written on them, he thought it best to finally come clean. This was the moment, the moment he feared. He had wanted to tell her in his own way and on his own terms, but that had been taken away from him.

She looked at the most recent telegram and asked, "What does cloudy mean? Who are you talking to?"

"If you let me see what you have, I'll explain everything," John urged.

"No, just answer my questions," she said.

Hearing them argue, Gabriel came downstairs and walked into the room. "Why are you yelling at each other?"

"Go back to your room. This is adult business," she said in a pleasant tone so as not to upset him.

"You're scaring me," he said, looking at them both, wide-eyed.

"Please, Gabriel, go back upstairs," Helen pleaded, her gentle tone cracking.

Gabriel hung his head low, turned and walked away.

After hearing his bedroom door close upstairs, Helen

continued, "What's your real name?"

John felt the pull between his feelings for her and his mission, but gave in because if he lied and was caught, he'd never get her back. "Nichols, my real last name is Nichols."

"John Nichols?"

"Yes."

"And who is Garrett Vane, and why are you sending him strange telegrams?" she asked.

"How do you know this? Who sent you that?" John asked.

"It doesn't matter who sent it. It all appears to be true; just answer the question," she insisted.

John was struggling. If he revealed the rest, who knew where this would go. She could easily understand and they would move on, or it could go off the rails. The Pinkerton Detective Agency didn't have a stellar reputation in St. Joseph.

"Answer me or leave. You know where the door is," she snapped, her arm shooting up and index finger pointing towards the front door.

"I work with him. We're partners," John blurted out.

"Work with him? Partners? In what?"

"I can't say much more. I don't want to put you in danger," John said, instantly regretting the word choice. "Wait, I didn't mean it like that."

"In danger, I just got out of danger, and now you're telling me you work or are partners with someone in Nashville, and if I know more, Gabriel and I are in danger? Really? After what we just went through?"

"Helen, please sit down, and I'll explain everything. I'll tell you everything, but please, I need you to understand, have an open heart and mind," John pleaded.

Helen's anger was welling up. She shook her head vigorously and under her breath kept repeating, "No, no, not again, no, not again."

John moved to walk around the table but stopped when she shouted at him to stop.

"Don't come near me!" she yelled.

"Helen, can I explain?"

"Explain, now, but I can't, I won't promise to understand. I've heard so many lies in my life. So many people have tried to hurt me, take what was mine. Remember those predators we talked about when I first met you? I meet you and think there's a good, honest man, well, not so honest. You're hiding something, something that you now say is dangerous," she said, rattling off her words in quick succession. "Were you ever married? Are you married now?"

"Helen, please, let me explain everything. I'll tell you everything, but please, I need you to sit down and remain calm."

Helen pulled a chair out and plopped down. "Go ahead, explain."

John took a seat across from her. He inhaled deeply then began, "My name is John Nichols. I am from Georgia, and upon my return from the war, I found my wife and daughter murdered. I then spent the next eleven years tracking down the men responsible. I ended up in Tucson; that's where I assumed the last name Smith. I needed to be secretive because I had good information that the man in charge, the one who ordered their murders, was there. While I was there, I became a deputy sheriff. I did this to help me gain a position to help me get this man. In the end, I found him. With that part of my life over, I went to Dodge City and found a position as a deputy marshal. After a month or more I was fired. I was then hired to protect a prominent banker and his son. We went to Deadwood. There I got tangled up in a conspiracy. I was arrested for a murder I didn't commit but was released when the real killer was found. There I met Garrett Vane, a Pinkerton agent—"

"Stop right there," Helen said, holding her hand out in front of her.

He knew what was coming next.

"Please tell me you're not a Pinkerton."

"Seeing how you put that, I wish I could say no, but that would be a lie. I am a Pinkerton," John confessed.

The life drained out of Helen's face. She put her head in her hands and began to weep.

"I'm sorry."

She wiped her tears and asked, "What are you doing in St. Joseph? Is it about the gold? Were you sent here like that bounty hunter to find me?"

Shocked by her comment, he quickly dashed her theory. "Heavens no. I'm not here for you at all."

"Finally some good news," she said, patting her chest with her hand and breathing deeply.

"Garrett and I were sent to track down the James brothers."

"That explains it," she said.

"Explains what?"

"You wanting to get to know me. This between us, it's all a ruse. You must know I know where they are, and you're hoping by getting close to me you'll find them."

"To be honest, at first I told myself that would be my excuse for violating my oath to the Pinkertons, because you're all I could think of the second I laid eyes on you. I calculated that you were a prominent woman in the county, and your husband had fought alongside the brothers, so you may know something. I didn't come to St. Joseph knowing who you were before."

"This...between us, these feelings you claim for me aren't real, then; they're phony, fake, all to get information on Jesse and Frank," she stated.

"You asked and I said no, not like that."

"I didn't ask. I stated a fact."

"But you're wrong. I met you and I swear I fell instantly in love with you. I felt guilty that I wasn't focused on my mission, so I justified my time and feelings for you as part of the job," John awkwardly explained.

"I was work for you?"

"No, I didn't say that."

"You just did."

"You're misunderstanding me," John said, once more regretting his choice of words.

Heavier tears welled in her eyes and broke free, streaming down her flushed cheeks.

It took every ounce of his restraint not to go and comfort her.

"I need you to leave, now," Helen barked.

"Please let me explain," John said, hoping to have more time to rephrase some of his statements.

"There's more?"

"No, that's it, but let me try to make you understand my position."

"Leave, go. Please don't make me get my rifle and force you out at gunpoint."

"You won't have to do that. I'll go peacefully. Can I get my things upstairs?" he asked, standing up from his seat.

"Yes, but hurry."

He walked towards the stairs, stopped and turned back towards her. He opened his mouth to talk but couldn't find the words. He'd destroyed everything; once more he'd made a mess of things. Thinking she needed some time to process, he raced up to his room, gathered his belongings and came back down. He found her still in the dining room crying. "May I pay a visit in a couple of days?"

"No."

"A letter?"

"If I want to see much less talk to you again, I'll contact you first," she snarled.

Her words were like a dagger to his heart.

"And just so you know, I do know where Jesse and Frank are, so I suppose I wasn't completely honest either when you asked about them days ago."

John didn't answer. He merely stood looking like a whipped dog.

"If they hear two Pinkertons are looking for them, you'll end up riddled with bullet holes in an unmarked grave. If I were you, I'd catch the next train back to wherever you came from."

His dagger to the heart turned into his heart being cut out of his chest. Maybe she was right, he should pack up and leave. His cover was blown, he was compromised, and here in front of him was a woman scorned. All it would take would be for her to tell them his name and where he might be; he'd be dead within an hour of that. Distraught, he turned and exited the house.

# CHAPTER SEVEN

"Honesty is the first chapter in the book of wisdom." –
Thomas Jefferson

## ST. JOSEPH, MISSOURI

## NOVEMBER 15, 1876

John exited the Western Union office empty-handed.
Concern welled up inside because he should have
received a telegram from Garrett in Nashville. Was he
okay? Had he been caught or, worse, killed? He didn't
think it a coincidence that after the situation with Helen,
he wasn't receiving any more telegrams from Garrett.
Who had sent her that envelope? What had been in it?
What did it say specifically? His frustration matched his
concern because he was filled with so many questions yet
had few answers. How long should he wait for a reply
before contacting the Chicago office, and was the
Western Union a confidential means of transmitting a
message? Had this office been compromised?

He staggered off down the street in the direction of
the hotel where he was staying. His body felt weighted
down by the lack of sleep. His nights were now restless as
he tossed and turned; his thoughts on Helen and how he
could get her back but equally on fulfilling his mission
and not getting killed. He remembered her stating she
knew where they were, but how could he ever get her to

reveal that sensitive information? Probably never was the answer he kept coming back to. With Helen, he had been so close to experiencing love again and one degree of separation from finding the James brothers. It was all gone now, and he didn't have any clue how to put it back together.

With his mind lost in thought, he didn't hear the heavy footfalls behind him until he was grabbed by the arm. John turned and raised his fist but relaxed when he saw it was Garrett. "What are you doing here?"

Garrett's jovial expression melted away. "You sent for me."

"No, I didn't," John replied.

"Yes, you did, two days ago," Garrett said, digging into his pocket and removing a small piece of paper. He handed it to John.

John took it and read. "I didn't send this," he replied. The paper in question was the telegram sent to Graham, which said SUNNY.

"Wait a minute, you didn't send this? How is that possible?" Garrett asked.

John looked around and said, "To my room, quick. Let's talk there."

The two rushed off towards the hotel.

\*\*\*

After John explained everything he knew, including his confession to Helen, Garrett was beyond angry. "Our entire mission is compromised. You're lucky you're still alive. Do you understand who we're dealing with? Huh? The Pinkertons don't have a good name in these parts because we killed their half-brother and maimed their mother. John, I brought you on, I vouched for you. What have you done?"

"She knows where they are; that's why I was pursuing her," he said, covering up his feelings for her.

"That doesn't matter now; you told her. For all you know, she could have told them," Garrett said, walking to the window and peeking out, his paranoia showing.

"If I give her some time, I think I may be able to convince her to tell me their whereabouts."

"Why in the hell would she do that? Give me one good reason why she'd reveal to you, a man she barely knows, the whereabouts of men who fought alongside her husband."

"Love."

"What?"

"You said one word, and that word is *love.*"

"I see what happened. You…you fell in love with her," Garrett said, pointing his finger at him as if he were a parent and John was his delinquent child.

"She has feelings for me."

"And you for her, just admit it. The sooner I know what exactly I'm dealing with, the quicker I can figure out a plan to get us out of it."

"Yes, I do," John finally admitted.

"Damn it, man, I need you thinking with your head not with your heart and especially not with that," Garrett said, now pointing at John's crotch.

"If you give me some time, I do believe I can win her trust back," John said with an air of confidence.

"She's not our only problem. Someone else knows we're here. You forget that someone outed us to her and even sent me a telegram using our code."

"The clerk at the Western Union."

"But you said he's just a kid, no older than nineteen."

"He is, but he would know. If we…say, persuade him to talk, you know, use some of our techniques for persuasion, we could get him to cough up who sent that telegram to you," John said.

Garrett thought for a minute, rubbing his chin and smoothing out his mustache with his thick fingers. "That could work. It would at least tell us who the other player on this chessboard is."

"Exactly," John said, grinning.

"What are we waiting for, then?" Garrett said, grabbing his hat.

The two raced down the stairs and were headed for the hotel exit when the front desk clerk called out, "Mr. Nance, oh, Mr. Nance."

John stopped and said, "Yes."

"A telegram was just delivered for you." The front desk clerk took a piece of paper from a small cubby and handed it to John.

Garrett and John gave each other a curious look before John opened the folded paper and read the telegram.

*YOUR SON IS DOING WELL. WE LONG TO SEE YOU SOON. DO NOT FORGET TO WRITE HIM*

*FOR HIS BIRTHDAY. MUCH LOVE – JOSIE*

John raised his brow and handed the telegram to Garrett. "It's gibberish."

Garrett scanned it and said, "No, it's not. It's a cipher." He rushed over to a small chair and sat. He removed a small notebook from his inside coat pocket, flipped through until he found the correct page, and began to decipher the message. Painstakingly, he worked, taking seconds to find each letter until he had the correct message.

"What does it say?"

"I won't bore you with the entire message, but we've been given another assignment."

"What?"

"More details will arrive in a parcel expected to arrive late today at the post office," Garrett said.

"We can't leave now," John said, urgency in his voice.

Garrett stood up, pocketed the letter and notebook, and said, "Don't fret. Until the package arrives, we continue our current job. Let's go talk to the clerk at the Western Union."

\*\*\*

The two crossed town quickly. When they reached the Western Union, they found a different clerk than normal working.

John asked, "The clerk who usually works here, he's young, say nineteen or twenty, brown hair and has a thin scar on his chin."

"You're looking for Edward," a middle-aged man replied, his tone eager and accommodating.

"Yes, Edward, where can we find him?" John asked.

"Unfortunately, Edward is home sick; came down with a chest cold. I expect him back to work the day after tomorrow."

"What's your name?" Garrett asked.

"Willard, sir."

"Willard, I really need to speak with him. Where does he live?" Garrett asked.

Growing uneasy, Willard replied, "Sir, it's not customary to give out the private addresses of our employees, I'm sorry. If there is some Western Union business you need from him, I can most certainly handle it."

"It's an emergency," John said, leaning over the counter.

Willard backed up a step and said, "Gentlemen, if there's no Western Union business you need, then please go. I find your questions, in fact your entire demeanor, a bit distressing."

Using his right hand, John pushed his coat aside and placed his hand on the back strap of his Colt. "If we were distressing, what is this?"

"Please go," Willard said, taking two more steps away from the counter.

The door opened behind them, and in came a woman and her young daughter. "Hello, Willard."

"Good morning, madam," Willard answered. He cut

a look at Garrett and John and said, "Goodbye, gentlemen."

Not wanting to create a scene in front of an innocent bystander, Garrett tugged at John's sleeve. Getting his attention, he said, "Let's go. We'll find him another way."

John nodded his agreement and the two exited the office. Back on the street, John said, "We should ask the businesses next door. Someone is bound to know where he lives."

"Good plan," Garrett said.

As the two were headed towards a tobacco shop, Graham spotted them from across the street. "John, hello, John!"

John spun around to see where the call was coming from. He stared across the bustling street and saw Graham waving. He returned a wave and said, "It's the sheriff."

Graham hurried towards them.

"He's coming," John said.

Garrett craned his head back and asked, "Tell me about the sheriff."

"Newly elected, in love with Helen, has a temper, and I'd venture he's corrupt," John said just in time as Graham cleared the distance and was now standing in front of them.

"Morning, John," Graham said, holding his hand out.

"Nice to see you, Sheriff," John said.

"Who's this?" Graham asked, although he suspected who it might be.

"Garrett Vane at your service," Garrett replied, holding his hand out.

Graham took Garret's hand and shook. "Nice to meet you. Say, what brings you to town?"

"Oh, um, visiting a friend," Garrett answered.

"That's nice. Listen, John, can I speak with you? It's quite urgent. It's about Helen," Graham said, wanting to get John and Garrett alone.

"Is something wrong with Helen?" John asked.

"How about you come to my office? Your friend can join us," Graham said.

John gave Garrett a glance to see if it was fine. Garrett replied with a nod.

The three men went to the sheriff's office. Inside, Graham took his usual seat at his desk, with John and Garrett sitting in the chairs on the far side.

Graham leaned back in his chair and folded his arms. With a devilish grin, Graham smiled but remained silent.

"Sheriff, what do you have to share with me concerning Helen?" John asked.

"So tell me, John, should I use Nance or Smith?" Graham asked, coming right out with the fact he knew John was hiding his true identity.

Shocked by Graham's question, John sat dumbfounded.

An awkward silence fell over the room.

After a minute Garrett shattered the quiet with a rhetorical question. "I assume you're the one who sent me the telegram?"

Graham gave Garrett a smile and said, "Yes. I'm

quite impressed that I figured out that code. You really need a more elaborate system."

"What do you want?" Garrett asked.

Leaning forward and jamming his index finger on the desk, Graham said, "This is my town. I'm the law here. Nothing happens in my town without me knowing. So whatever you two have going on, this is your time to come clean, or God help me, I'll arrest you both."

John sat without saying a word. He let Garrett take the lead on answering these questions.

"What would you like to know?" Garrett asked.

"Did you not hear me? I'm the law; you tell me everything," Graham said.

Garrett sighed and shook his head. As he reached into his coat, Graham jumped. "Hold it right there!" Pulling his hand back, Garrett said, "I'm just grabbing a cigar."

"Go ahead," Graham said.

Garrett pulled the cigar from his pocket and prepared it for smoking. As he did this, he explained the situation to Graham in the simplest of terms. "Sheriff, we've been sent here from the Pinkerton Detective Agency to find a couple of outlaws."

"Who?"

"That is confidential," Garrett said.

"Were you not listening? Tell me everything or I throw you in jail."

Garrett lit his cigar, took several long drags, and blew a plume of smoke into the air. "By telling you, we could possibly be putting you in danger."

"This is your last chance. Next time you avoid me, you go to jail, and believe me, I'll have you in there for weeks, maybe months, before a trial date," Graham warned.

"We're here to track and capture Frank and Jesse James," Garrett reluctantly confessed.

John suddenly remembered Helen telling him that Graham wasn't a trustworthy person; he now hoped that the information Garrett was sharing wouldn't be used against them.

"What is it with everyone coming to my town with hopes of capturing those brothers?" Graham asked.

"Sheriff, you can assist us in this mission if you'd like. I'm sure our main office in Chicago would approve," Garrett offered, hoping the allure of working with them would alleviate any issues with divulging their mission to the sheriff.

"You need help?"

"We can always use help," Garrett replied.

"Is there pay involved?" Graham asked.

"I can certainly ask Chicago; but usually our law enforcement partners don't charge us for their assistance," Garrett explained.

"Let me think about the offer. So have you fellas had any success?"

"Not yet," John blurted out.

Graham shifted his attention to John and asked, "Does Helen know you're a Pinkerton?"

"Yes."

"And how did she take the news? I can imagine she

wasn't happy to find out your true identity. You know I warned her about you, told her not to trust you; it appears I was correct in my assessment," Graham gloated.

"It was you that sent those notes and telegrams to Helen, wasn't it?" John asked.

"Yes, it was me. I've known Helen for years; she deserves better than someone who can't be honest about who they really are."

"You know something, I agree; she does deserve better than me or you," John sniped.

Graham gritted his teeth and said, "Is there anything else I should know? I suggest you tell me everything, 'cause if I find out you're not telling the truth, you'll go straight to jail."

Unable to reveal more, Garrett lied, "That's it."

Knowing Garrett lied for a reason, John kept his mouth shut.

"Gentlemen, I'll consider your offer for assistance, and next time the Pinkerton Detective Agency wishes to send people to my county, I'd appreciate a heads-up," Graham said in a scolding tone.

"I'll be sure to pass this information on," Garrett said, standing.

John followed suit, gripping his hat tightly in his hands.

"And, John, I suggest you stay away from Helen. Word is she's quite upset," Graham snarled.

Keeping his head and wits about him, John didn't utter a word in response to Graham.

"Sheriff, please do us a favor and keep our identities

confidential. It's bad enough you exposed us to Mrs. Mills," Garrett said before he headed to the door, with John following.

"Mr. Vane, you can be assured that no other person will be apprised of your true identities, and may I ask when you think you'll be wrapping up your manhunt? I ask because you must feel vulnerable knowing that a woman with Mrs. Mills's past associations might…talk."

"We're discussing that now," Garrett answered.

"Please do tell me when you plan on leaving," Graham said, opening the front door and holding it wide for them to leave.

"Good day, Sheriff," Garrett said, his temper rising with each second.

The two exited but didn't step off the walkway. They stood and stared at the people coming and going down the street. The revelation that Graham was the one behind leaking their identities was troubling to say the least. Having the head law enforcement officer in the town against them only complicated their objectives and put into jeopardy the missions themselves.

"Now what?" John asked.

"You go back to the hotel and wait for the parcel. I'm heading to Western Union to send a message to Chicago informing them we've been compromised."

"Aren't you worried your message will be intercepted? This office can't be trusted," John said.

"I know, and I plan on using that to our advantage," Garrett said and rushed off down the street.

\*\*\*

Taking hold of the whiskey, Graham stared at the slick sides of the glass, wet from overpouring the shot. He admired the brown hue of the liquor, its color reminding him of his mother's eyes. His mind raced to a memory of her when he was twelve. He had returned from school, tears streaming down his flushed cheeks and snot hanging from his nose. On his bloodied elbows and knees were the signs of a scuffle. The last thing he wanted to do was have her see him in this condition, so he entered the house and sprinted up the stairs, but his mother was never one for being ignored. Curious as to why Graham hadn't stopped to greet her, she went to his bedroom to find him surrounded by bloodstained rags. Concerned, she asked what had happened. Graham wouldn't talk. After much coaxing, Graham confided that he'd been bullied by several boys, resulting in his being thrown to the ground and kicked. She then proceeded to tell him one of the most valuable lessons he'd ever learn. In a very calm voice she said, "Fight back. Even if you might lose…always fight back."

He took her words to heart and did as she said. He eventually would define fighting back in his own terms. Sometimes it meant punishing your enemies in creative ways, or attacking their means or business. And tonight he planned on keeping the fight going against John. He had him on the ropes; now was the time to finish him off.

Just as he went to toss back the celebratory shot, Byron appeared. "Sheriff Hooper, I see you're enjoying yourself."

Graham nodded and promptly drank the shot. "Bartender, two more."

"I won't be drinking tonight, so no, thank you," Byron said, waving off the bartender as he approached with a fresh glass and the bottle. He glanced around the barroom of the Great Ox and said, "I should really open up a bar. If it wasn't against the law to drink on Sunday, I swear this place would be packed seven days a week."

"Drink with me," Graham said.

"I have an early day tomorrow, so no," Byron said then shifted the topic. "Listen, Graham, about the other day—"

"Stop, don't say it. I can hear in your voice that you're about to say you're sorry. I'm the one who needs to apologize for my behavior, not you," Graham said, patting Byron on the shoulder.

"But I should too," Byron said.

"If you do, I won't accept it," Graham snorted, filling the two glasses and sliding one close to Byron. He picked his up and said, "Go ahead, pick it up. Toast with me."

"So we're celebrating something?" Byron said, making an exception and taking the glass in his hand.

"To winning," Graham said, tapping Byron's glass. He drank the shot and slammed the glass down hard on the wooden bar.

Byron drank his and said, "What did you win?"

"My dignity, I've gotten it back," Graham replied.

"I didn't know you lost it, my friend," Byron joked,

but his mind was troubled by what he'd heard.

"How long have we been friends? Twenty-some odd years?" Graham asked.

"Twenty-three to be exact. We met in school," Byron answered.

"That's right. See, you always know the specifics; you're good about that. You know stuff; it's one of the things I admire about you," Graham said. "I'm going to need your help. I'm going to need some of that knowledge in order to outright win this entire thing."

"What are you winning? Who are you competing with?" Byron asked, genuinely curious and concerned by Graham's word usage.

Ignoring his questions, Graham continued, "You have little spies in town, you know things that you shouldn't, you get information. I need some information that I think you may be able to get me."

"Spies? Oh, come on, Graham, you're making me out to be someone I'm not," Byron countered.

"Byron, don't deny it. I admire that in you," Graham said, reaching over and taking hold of Byron's arm. "Are you my friend?"

"Of course, one of your oldest and closest," Byron confirmed sincerely.

"Then I need you to do me the biggest favor. I need you to use all your resources, all those little spies, and get some information to someone."

"Who do you need to contact that you, the sheriff, can't?" Byron asked.

Graham leaned in and whispered, "I need you to

pass a message to Jesse James."

# CHAPTER EIGHT

"If there is no struggle, there is no progress." – Frederick
Douglass

## MILLS FARM, ST. JOSEPH, MISSOURI

## NOVEMBER 16, 1876

The parcel had arrived, and it contained all the details
John and Garrett needed to know. Their job was to
augment the security already on the train. The cargo
contained on one of the cars was old United States
Treasury notes set to be properly destroyed back in
Washington, DC. The destruction of these old notes was
a term set in the Resumption Act passed by Congress in
1875.

The catch was the notes were being transported via a
passenger train, which wasn't an uncommon practice.
John and Garrett were to travel to Lawrence, Kansas, and
meet the train on November 19. They'd be remaining
undercover and board the train as passengers. According
to some raw intelligence received by an undercover
Pinkerton agent in Kansas City, the train was vulnerable
on the stretch of track from Lawrence to Kansas City.
There was no other information on who might be
contemplating robbing the train, but the intelligence
proved quality enough for Chicago to order additional
security for that route.

With their new mission, Garrett and John planned on leaving on November 17 and riding by horseback to Lawrence. Until then, they agreed to lie low and stay in their rooms. This was something that was difficult for John. He hadn't seen nor heard from Helen in days and wanted more than anything to see her before he left. Disregarding his own safety, he decided he would sneak out and attempt to see her; so under the protection of twilight, he set out. The entire ride he thought of how he'd again try to explain himself and prayed she'd listen this time. He hoped she'd used their time apart to fully see he wasn't the man she should be afraid of. Regardless of what he prayed or hoped for, soon he'd know.

When the few lights from her house came into view, his stomach tightened. How would she respond to him? Would she throw him out like before? So many questions peppered his thoughts. He hated the wait and prodded the horse to trot faster.

Arriving at the house, he looked and saw her passing by a window. He paused and began to question his decision to come. Was he making a mistake? Would this backfire? Brushing aside the doubtful thoughts, he dismounted and stepped up to the front door. He knocked and waited patiently.

"Who's there?' Helen called out from the other side of the closed door.

"It's John."

A long pause.

"Helen, it's John. Can we talk?"

"I told you that I'd come to you," she shot back.

"I'm leaving tomorrow, not sure when I'll return. I wanted to see you before I left," he confessed.

She unlocked the door, opened it enough to peek out, and asked, "You're leaving?"

John removed his hat and replied, "Yes, and I couldn't go without seeing you again and telling you that I'm truly sorry for lying to you. It wasn't meant to hurt you. Had I known, had God given me the foresight to see you were in my future, I'd never have taken the job with Pinkerton and would have come directly here."

"Is that all?" she asked.

"I also wanted to tell you that I love you," he replied. He thought about how odd it was to hear those words come from his lips.

"You don't lie to someone you claim to love," she said.

"But I..." he said and stopped himself. He decided he wasn't going to argue with her. "You're right, but you should know that I intended to tell you, I was looking for the right time. I suppose I should have just trusted that you would hear without judging me."

"I would have judged, but had you told me without being outed, I might not have asked you to leave," Helen confessed.

John cursed to himself that he hadn't done so, but it was too late now. He was standing there dealing with the consequences of his actions. "How's Gabriel?"

"He's getting better every day," Helen answered.

John prayed she'd let him inside, but it appeared, as each second ticked away, that wasn't going to be the case.

"If that is all you have to say, I'll need to bid you goodnight," Helen said.

"Please tell me at least you'll consider forgiving me and giving me a chance again to win your heart," John pleaded.

"I thought you were leaving," Helen said.

"I am, but if I know we have a chance, I'll return but not as a Pinkerton. I'll resign my position for you," he pledged.

She looked down and sighed.

"Please let me prove I can be the man you need."

"I'll consider it, that's all," she said, looking back up, their eyes meeting.

As if shot full of adrenaline, John perked up and said, "You will?"

"I said consider; I make no promises."

"I understand, thank you," John said. He wanted to give her a kiss but knew that was asking too much from her.

"Now leave me, the hour is getting late, and I need to go to bed," Helen said.

"Good night," John said.

Helen closed the door, leaving John engulfed in the dark of night but full of promise that there was still hope for them to be together.

## TWENTY-TWO MILES SOUTH OF ST. JOSEPH, MISSOURI

The canvas bag covering Graham's head made it

impossible to see but also difficult to breathe. What started as excitement this morning was now fear. When Byron had come to him that morning and said his inquiries concerning the James brothers had already borne fruit, he was shocked, but what he now found more shocking was how he was being treated. He was first instructed to ride north out of town to an abandon homestead; there he found instructions written for him to put the bag over his head and wait. A short while later someone arrived, tied his arms behind his back, and placed him in a wagon. For what seemed like an eternity, he was driven to an unknown location, where he now sat, waiting and worrying. Around him he heard unintelligible chatter, but no one acknowledged him; it was as if he weren't there.

"Hello," Graham cried out. "I can't breathe that well with this thing over my head."

Laughter broke out.

"I'm the sheriff of Buchanan County. I order you to remove this bag from my head!" he wailed in anger.

"Listen here, Sheriff, we'll remove the bag when we're told. Now just sit there and be patient," a man replied, his voice filled with joy, no doubt at the sight of Graham being humiliated.

"I'm through with this. Take me back. I don't wish to make a deal," Graham declared. He listened for a response, but nothing came. The sound of a door opening and closing hit his ears. "Hello? Are you there?"

The door opened.

"Hello, anyone there?" Graham called out.

Footfalls drew close.

Graham could hear and feel someone close. "Hello."

Without notice, the bag was ripped off his head. Graham blinked repeatedly and looked around. He found himself in a barn; nothing looked familiar. He looked down and saw barbed wire fencing tools spread out on a table. Glancing up, he saw a middle-aged bearded man standing above him. He blinked a few more times until his vision cleared and asked, "Are you...Jesse James?"

"I am," Jesse answered.

Two more men came into the barn and stood feet behind Jesse. In their hands they held hatchets.

"Why am I here? Why have you taken me here? This meeting should have been done with a mutual understanding and respect for my office," Graham sniveled.

"Respect? Have you forgotten who I am? I don't hold much respect for people such as yourself." Jesse laughed. "Did you think we were going to sit down over a roast and brandy and talk? This isn't a negotiation, this is an interrogation."

"What? No, I sent word that I had information I wanted to sell, information that led to two Pinkerton agents in town."

Jesse turned around and faced the two men and began to laugh loudly. Seconds later, the other men began to laugh. "Can you believe this? He thought he was coming here to sell me something."

"I was. That's the message I sent."

"Sheriff, you're mistaken. The message I received

said you were working with two Pinkerton agents to track me down. Now you must know I don't care much for Pinkertons, especially after what they did to my mother and my stepbrother," Jesse seethed.

A look of utter terror washed over Graham's face. His eyes darted around the room, hoping to spot anything that could give him hope, something that could give him a hint that escape was possible or a weapon placed somewhere he could easily use.

Jesse reached down and took a handful of Graham's hair. He jerked his head back and said, "Tell me where those Pinkertons are."

"For a price. Let me go and I'll tell you," Graham cried out.

Jesse waved.

One of the men stepped up, put down his hatchet, and picked up a rusty wire cutter.

"What are you doing?" Graham asked as he struggled to free himself from the bindings behind his back.

Jesse pounded the table and barked, "Do it."

The man walked behind Graham, pulled his pinkie finger free, and cut it off.

Graham howled in pain. Tears burst from his eyes as he wailed, "Argh! What are you doing? I'm the sheriff of—"

Jesse pounded the table and hollered, "I don't give a damn who you are. You're nothing but a traitor. I know you, I know what you did during the war. You took advantage of the poor folk of the area and bought their land for pennies on the dollar when they couldn't afford to keep them up. You didn't fight for the cause; no, you actively worked against it. When I got word that you were working with the Pinkertons and that you wanted to talk, I knew I had my chance and the moral grounds to finally put an end to you."

"I'm not working with the Pinkertons. I wanted to sell you the information that they were here. Byron lied, he lied."

"I don't know who Byron is," Jesse barked. "Now tell me, where can I find your compatriots?"

"Let me go. I'll tell you," Graham pleaded.

Jesse looked at his man, who pulled another finger free and severed it from Graham's hand.

"Argh! What are you doing?" Graham crowed.

"Where are your friends?" Jesse shouted.

"Promise me you'll let me go," Graham begged.

"Another finger," Jesse ordered.

Graham tried to stand up but was shoved back down. The other man came over and assisted as another finger was cut off.

"No! Stop it, please. I beg you," Graham cried.

"Where are they?" Jesse asked.

"No more, please, don't cut off any more fingers. I'll tell you where they are, and I'll tell you about Helen Mills too." Graham pleaded.

Jesse stood erect and cocked his head after hearing Helen's name. "Tell me what about Helen Mills?"

"She and one of the Pinkertons, a John Smith—that's his real name; he's been using Nance around here—but that isn't the point, the point is he and she are in love.

They're romantically involved," Graham confessed.

"I don't believe that," Jesse replied.

"They are, I swear it," Graham said.

"Take another finger," Jesse ordered.

Before the man could, Graham cried out, "I swear it on my life. They're in love. I've seen them kiss with my own eyes."

Jesse held up his hand, gesturing for his man not to remove another finger. "You swear?"

"I swear. No more fingers. Promise me you'll not cut off any more fingers if I tell you where the two Pinkertons are," Graham said.

"I'm a Southern gentleman. My word is my bond." Jesse smiled.

"They're staying at the Blossom Hotel in St. Joseph, rooms six and eight," Graham said, his breathing rapid as the shock and blood loss were forcing his body into shock.

"Good man," Jesse said, leaning over the table and patting Graham on the top of his sweaty head. He looked at his men and ordered, "Send two men to get Helen Mills and bring her here, they're not to harm her, and you two go bring those Pinkertons back here. It's okay to rough them up, but don't kill them unless you have to."

"What about me?" Graham asked.

"You're staying here for the moment. If I find out you're lying, I'll kill you myself," Jesse said. He turned and exited the barn, leaving Graham whimpering.

# CHAPTER NINE

"Do I not destroy my enemies when I make them my
friends?" – Abraham Lincoln

## TWENTY-TWO MILES SOUTH OF ST. JOSEPH,
MISSOURI

## NOVEMBER 17, 1876

The newspapers and serial novellas all put Jesse James at
six feet or more with a presence that was bigger than his
stature. After having met him, John could attest that, for
once, the newspapers were correct.

John didn't know what he was about to encounter in
the house. Having only just woken from being kidnapped,
he was feeling out of place. In the span of ten minutes
he'd awakened in a dark cell with his partner, had met the
notorious and infamous outlaws Jesse and Frank James,
and had struck a deal with them to steal United States
Treasury notes from a train in two days. His life had
become the dime novels he'd read.

Jesse confidently walked into the brightly lit house,
leaving the door open behind him.

John stepped in and was instantly hit by the smell of
pipe smoke and the stench of mold. He looked around
the room to find no furnishings, only crates.

Jesse passed through that room and into the kitchen.
"Get in here."

John followed, ensuring he took in every detail of the house and items in view in case he needed that information for later. Once in the kitchen, John found an oval table with six chairs. The tabletop was scratched and worse for wear. The walls were bare, telling him the house was abandoned, a perfect hideout for two outlaws on the run.

"Take a seat," Jesse said, snapping his fingers and pointing towards a chair.

John did exactly as he said but did take the seat where his back was against the wall.

Jesse disappeared up the stairs.

John heard people talking but couldn't make out what they were saying. It was evident now that someone else was in the house other than them. Who could he want him to meet? John asked himself. It was a strange reply.

Heavy footfalls on the wooden steps told him someone was coming downstairs. John could only assume it was Jesse and this mystery person. Anxious, John sat erect in his chair and waited.

"He's in the kitchen," Jesse said.

From around the corner, Helen appeared. She motioned ever so slightly to John with a head shake before she said, "Yes, I know this man. His name is John Nance."

John understood her subtle suggestion and remained quiet.

Helen turned and faced Jesse, who came back into the room and stood next to her. "He worked on Daniel

Askew's farm, and he helped me rescue Gabriel from that bounty hunter; but to say I'm romantically involved with him is nonsense. As far as knowing if he's a Pinkerton agent, that's news to me."

Jesse nodded and said, "I trust you, Helen. We've been through a lot together, and you were a big help during the uprising in sixty-six. So if you tell me you're not involved with this man, I believe it."

"Can I go home now?" Helen asked.

"Gabriel will be fine. One of my men is looking over him. I swear to you no harm will come to the boy."

"I know you won't hurt him. Just after what happened, he's more fragile than normal," Helen said.

"The sheriff, he's the one," Jesse said.

"The one what?" Helen asked.

"He's the one who implicated you and them," Jesse said, turning away and calling out, "Go get the sheriff."

At the far end of the house, the door could be heard opening then closing. A few minutes later it opened again. From the front room, Graham appeared. His trousers were soaked with blood, and his face was ashen.

Upon seeing Helen and John in the same room, he cried out, "Right there, they, she, he's a Pinkerton and she's in love with that bastard." Graham stumbled forward, his arms still bound behind his back. He ran into the table and almost fell over. "I told you they're in love. Now let me go."

"He doesn't look well," Helen said.

"That's because we cut off two of his fingers. He's bled quite a bit." Jesse laughed.

"What are you going to do with him?" Helen asked.

Graham looked at Helen and snarled, "I hate you! I hope he skins you alive!"

"I told him if he lied, I'd kill him," Jesse said and pulled out a Colt. He cocked it and aimed it at Graham's head.

"No, you said…" Graham cried out.

"Jesse, wait," Helen gasped.

With a slight pressure on the trigger, the pistol fired. The .45-caliber round struck Graham in the forehead and sent him reeling backwards into the wall. He slid down and hit the floor dead.

Helen stepped back, her hand covering her mouth in shock at what she'd just witnessed.

Jesse's reputation was that of a ruthless man, and once more, the newspapers had it right, John thought.

"I said I was a man of my word, and let this be a lesson to you, Mr. Nichols, and to you, Helen, that if I find out you lied, that will be your fate," Jesse said, holstering the pistol.

***

Jesse decided to keep Helen there while he decided whether she was truthful or not. The killing of Graham was simply a way of disposing of a man he despised and a shocking way to send John and Helen a message.

Unable to sleep, Helen lay on an old mattress in the upstairs bedroom where they were holding her. Once more in a matter of days she and Gabriel were in a life-or-death situation. This time she could say it had to do with John, but her real issue went all the way back to her allegiance and alliance with the James brothers after the war. Taking the gold was her first mistake; then helping them and conspiring against the government back then was her second. She remembered Jesse, but not like this. He was a hard man, a tough man, but now he was a cold-blooded murderer.

She had a lot to dislike about Graham and had even thought about killing him herself, but actually seeing it was something else. He was a bad person, but being tortured then executed was a brutal way to go, she thought. Her thoughts then drifted back to Gabriel and what he must be thinking if he were awake. She couldn't wait for Jesse to make up his unstable mind. No, she needed to act and fast or she'd never see Gabriel again. She sat up and said under her breath, "I need to get out of here."

\*\*\*

John could see the glow of dawn making its appearance to the east. He was utterly exhausted and wanted nothing more than to sleep, but Jesse and Frank had kept him up all night detailing a plan on how to get the treasury notes from the train down to John's contact in Texas.

Several times Jesse had asked him for the name of his contact, but John wouldn't give it. He needed some leverage to keep him alive long enough to see another dawn.

"Well, Jesse, it sounds like we need to use him," Frank said.

"I don't like it. Once he's on that train, what will keep him from outing our plan to the law or other Pinkertons?" Jesse said.

"I'm right here, and you need to know I won't out you," John said.

Frank pulled Jesse into the other room to discuss it out of earshot; however, John was able to pick up a few key words like *kill*, *other guy* and *dynamite*. John recalled seeing the crates upon entering the house and now assumed they were dynamite. Using such an explosive wasn't out of the ordinary for outlaws to open safes or derail trains, so it made sense. Hearing *kill* and *other guy* must have meant that Garrett's life was in danger; the deal he struck was probably not going to be held to, and why would it? Garrett was correct earlier when he said you couldn't make deals with men like them.

Frank and Jesse returned and said, "Here's what's going to happen. You and Jesse will ride to Lawrence; there he'll pretend to be your partner. We'll set up just west of Linwood. You and Jesse will place dynamite on the coupler of the train car with the notes and the passengers. Once it's blown, it will separate the car from the engine and other cars. We'll be there with wagons to take the notes to a barge we'll have on the Arkansas River just south. From there we'll take the river down into Indian Territory—"

"Some people call it Oklahoma," Jesse interrupted.

Annoyed, Frank asked, "Does it matter what we call

it?"

Jesse shrugged his shoulders.

"We'll need wagons once we disembark down here. We'll take the notes the rest of the way overland to your man in Dallas," Frank said, his finger following along a route marked on a map.

"I'll be coming with you to Dallas. It's the only way he'll do business with you," John insisted.

"This is where I disagree," Jesse said.

"He may be right," Frank said.

"What if he's lyin'?" Jesse said.

"And if he is, we'll find out in a couple of days. Until then we go with this plan," Frank said. "Say, how much in notes do you reckon is on that car?" Frank asked John.

"Not sure, but if I were a betting man, and I am, I'd say millions."

Jesse's and Frank's eyes widened at the thought.

"What my friend in Dallas will give you is up for negotiation, though," John said.

Frank yawned and stretched. "Time for some shut-eye. I suggest you get some too, brother."

Jesse nodded. "Agreed. I'll get one of the guys to watch the two here."

"You're leaving? You're not staying here?" John asked, seeing them head for the front door.

"Hell no, we're not staying here, but you are. You best get some rest. We've got a long ride to Lawrence later today," Jesse said, closing the front door with Frank just ahead of him.

A second later the door opened, and in stepped one

of their men armed with two Colts on his hip. In his arms he held a blanket. He walked over to John and tossed it at him. "Sleep tight." He laughed as he walked into the other room, sat down in a chair, and put his feet up.

John took the blanket and laid it on the floor as far away from Graham's body as he could. The fact that his body still lay there was repulsive. It didn't take John long to fall asleep; within seconds he was out cold.

\*\*\*

"Wake up!" Helen hollered, pushing John hard.

John opened his eyes and shot up. "Helen, what's going on?"

"We're getting out of here now. Come, hurry," Helen urged, towering over him with a pistol in each hand.

Not hesitating, John sprang to his feet and looked around. His eyes stopped on the guard, who now had a hatchet buried in his head. "Did you do that?"

"No time to talk. We need to leave. There's horses out back," Helen said, giving him one of the pistols. She rushed towards the back door and threw it open.

"Garrett, we can't leave Garrett!" John exclaimed. "He's locked in the barn!"

"We don't have time to get him," Helen said but stopped short of leaving, as a man was coming towards her. She slammed the door shut and turned to John. "Someone's coming!"

"Open up!" the man shouted as he banged on the door.

"Out the front, come," John said, taking her hand. The two ran through the house to the front door. John cracked the door open to see two other men were standing there. "Damn it!"

Gunfire came from the back followed by the back door bursting open. "Where are ya?" the man called out.

John cocked the Colt and stepped into the front room to get a clear view of the back just in time, as the man was coming towards him. John squeezed the trigger, placing a well-aimed round into the man's chest.

The man dropped to his knees and fell over dead.

"Helen, the back might be clear now. Come on," John said, again taking her hand.

A volley of bullets suddenly rained down on the small house, many of the rounds penetrating the dry rotten siding and whizzing past them. One round struck a kerosene lantern, causing it to explode, splashing kerosene and flames all over the front room where the dynamite was.

John and Helen reached the back, but once more were prevented from exiting as two more men appeared, guns pointed at them and firing. "Son of a bitch!" John cried out in frustration. "We need to get out of this house before it blows."

"What?" Helen asked, taking cover behind the door jamb.

"The crates in the front room are filled with dynamite," John said.

"How many are there?" Helen asked.

"Four, I think. I believe we drew the men from the

barn up here," John answered. He crawled to a window that overlooked the back of the house and peered out. He spotted one man behind the old well and another positioned behind the outhouse. He cocked the pistol, took aim, and shot the man at the outhouse. His aim was true, and the man toppled over. "Make that three now."

The fire had reached up and was fully engulfing the ceiling and exposed beams that supported it. The heat was becoming intense and unbearable for Helen and John, and with the dynamite just lying on the floor surrounded by open flame, it was only a matter of time before it exploded.

"We've got to make a run for it. We'll go out the back, make for the horses," John said.

Helen nodded.

"Give me your pistol," John said, holding his left hand out, palm up.

"Won't I need it?" Helen asked.

"I'm going to cover you using both. Get to the horses as fast as your legs will take you. As soon as you mount, ride, get out of here. I'll then go, get a horse, and make for the barn. I can't leave Garrett."

Helen leaned in and kissed him.

"What was that for?" he asked, surprised.

"I love you. I wanted you to hear it just in case we don't make it out of here," Helen said.

"I love you too," John replied. "Now on a count of three."

Helen crawled to the door and lifted the handle.

"One," he said, cocking both pistols. "Two," he said,

standing ready just behind the door, and, "Three."

Helen threw open the door.

John stood in the open doorway and began firing at the well. He then noticed that the other two men had made their way around and were also taking cover there. Determined, he stood his ground and fired.

Helen dashed out. She reached a horse, untied it from a post, and jumped on. She kicked it hard and sprinted off towards the barn.

The gunfire spooked the other two horses, causing them to rear and break free. Within seconds they had run off.

One by one, John picked off the men.

Knowing John wanted her to leave, she knew how he felt about Garrett. She bounded off the horse when she reached the barn and ran inside. "Garrett?" she cried out.

"Here!" Garrett replied.

She unlatched the heavy door and pushed it open.

Garrett stepped out and said, "You must be Helen."

"Come, John needs help," she said.

Back at the house, John was still fighting. He'd killed all but one but was down to one remaining round.

The man hiding behind the well rose to shoot, but John was steady and drilled him with his last bullet to the chest. As he stepped from the cover of the door jamb, a beam fell from the ceiling and struck him in the head, knocking him down. He fell from the open doorway and onto the ground, unconscious.

Helen and Garrett exited the barn. She looked up

towards the house but didn't see John, nor did she hear gunfire anymore. "Where is he?"

The house suddenly exploded with massive force, throwing fiery debris three hundred and sixty degrees and a hundred yards out. The concussion from the blast was so powerful Helen and Garrett were thrown to the ground. She got up quickly and looked towards what remained of the house. "John, no!"

# EPILOGUE

"We must let go of the life we have planned, so as to accept the one that is waiting for us." – Joseph Campbell

## CHICAGO, ILLINOIS

## DECEMBER 2, 1876

John woke to find he was in a hospital bed. The intense daylight coming in from the window was blinding. He looked around but didn't recognize anyone, nor could he recall how he'd gotten there or what day it was. With a trembling hand, he reached up to touch his head and found a thick bandage wrapped around it. When he lowered his right arm, he then noticed his arms were covered in bandages as well. Confused and growing agitated on why and how he'd ended up where he was and with the injuries he'd sustained, he cried out, "Help, anyone, help!"

A young woman dressed in a long white dress rushed over. "What is it?"

"Are you a nurse?" he asked even though it was obvious based upon her attire.

"Yes, I'm this ward's head nurse. How can I help you? Is something wrong?"

"Where am I?" he asked.

A bewildered look appeared on her face as she replied, "Why, this is Cook County Hospital."

Hearing the name startled him, as he'd never heard of it before. He tried to sit up, but a searing pain shot through his body.

"Sir, you must remain still. Your injuries were substantial. It's amazing you're even alive," the nurse said.

He glanced out the window closest to him and noticed buildings all around. He was in a big city, but where? "Are we in Kansas City?"

The nurse chuckled and replied, "Heavens no, we're in Chicago."

"Chicago? How is that possible? What happened?"

She cocked her head and asked, "You really don't remember a thing?"

"If I did, would I be asking?" he snarled.

The nurse pursed her lips and shot back, "Don't take a tone. It's not appreciated."

"I apologize, I'm just confused. The last thing I remember was I was on a train..." he said, pausing to concentrate. He raised his arm again and touched his head. "It hurts."

"The doctor said it would for some time. You took quite a blow to the head; like I said, it's a miracle you're still alive."

"How did I get here?" he asked.

"Not quite sure, all I know is your employer is paying the bills," she said.

"Pinkerton?"

She took a clipboard from the end of the bed and looked at it. "Yes, Pinkerton Detective Agency."

He pressed his eyes closed tightly and tried to focus

his blurry thoughts. "Garrett…Garrett Vane, has he been by?"

"You've had a few visitors. I don't recall any names though. Mr. Nichols, I think you should rest some more."

Suddenly a terrible thought popped in his head. He lifted the sheets to ensure his legs were still there. Seeing them, he breathed a sigh of relief. "Thank God."

"Fearful your legs wouldn't be there?" she quipped.

"Yes."

"You're intact, well, except your memory, it seems. I can ask the doctor about that, but my experience is that memory returns after a period of time. You suffered severe trauma to the head, jostled your brain a bit." She laughed.

Not finding his situation humorous, he asked, "Can I see the doctor?"

"He's busy now, but I'll let him know you're finally awake and talking."

Finding part of her response curious, he asked, "Wait. How long have I been unconscious?"

"Oh, Mr. Nichols, my dear man, you've been here for almost two weeks."

John's face turned ashen, and a queasiness began to grow inside him.

"You don't look well. Will you be needing a bucket?"

He waved her off and said, "Just leave me alone. Go, please."

"As you wish," the nurse said, walking away.

John felt like his world was falling all around him. He'd awakened into a world that resembled more of a nightmare. Questions came at him in quick succession. He was confused and distraught, but at least he was alive, he thought. Whatever had happened or whoever had tried to kill him, it had failed. He slumped deeper into the bed, pressed his eyes closed, and drifted back to a time that he could recall with clarity.

Each time he'd get to a time period about a month ago; then everything would get foggy. Growing agitated, he opened his eyes and cursed loudly.

The nurse who had attended him earlier and another shot him an annoyed look and signaled for him to remain quiet.

Not known for his obedience, he tossed off the sheets. Anticipating his next action would bring pain, he counted to three then swung his legs out. The pain was immense, but not enough to persuade him to stay in the bed. Seeing a cane hanging from the bed next to him, he grabbed it and used it to help him get to his feet.

He looked left and right up the long rectangular ward, the walls lined with twin-sized beds, all occupied with people suffering various injuries or diseases. To his right he spotted a double set of swinging doors. That was the exit, and he was getting out of there. His first step was incredibly painful, with the second even more. His hope was that with each new step the pain would subside; by his sixth step he found that theory was wrong.

"Wait, Mr. Nichols, you can't leave. Wait!" the nurse hollered from the far side of the long ward.

Her cry for him to stop only served to motivate him to move faster. When he reached the double doors, the nurse was not far behind. He went to push, but his timing was off. The door swung inwards and hit him squarely in the face and sent him tumbling to the floor.

"Oh no," the nurse cried out, concerned for his well-being.

John grunted in pain but was determined to leave. He struggled to get to his feet but was having the most difficult time doing it.

"You look like a fish out of water, flopping all around," a familiar voice boomed above him.

John looked up and saw it was Garrett. "Wait, you're here."

"Of course I am. I've been visiting you daily," Garrett said, reaching down and offering a hand. "C'mon, let's get you to your feet and put you back in bed."

The nurse helped while giving John an earful. "Mr. Nichols, you cannot be conducting yourself this way. This is a respectable hospital and there are patients who want to be here. Your actions are deplorable."

"I see you haven't changed," Garrett quipped.

John gave him a confused look and replied, "It's so good to see you."

Garrett and the nurse escorted John back to his bed.

When he was back in and comfortable, John fired off a volley of questions.

Garrett held up his hands and said, "One at a time."

The nurse rolled her eyes and snapped, "Keep your friend under control, please."

"I'll do my best," Garrett said with a devilish grin.

The nurse strutted off.

"I can't remember anything. I'm so confused. I don't understand what happened, how I got here, and how this happened," he said, holding up his bandaged arms.

"I don't mind telling you, but you need to relax, take a deep breath, and settle down," Garrett said.

"How can I settle down? The last blurry thing I remember was being on a train, but I'll be honest, I don't know if that memory is from when I arrived in St. Joseph or it's another memory. I have a foggy memory of a farm too."

Reaching out and gently tapping his shoulder, Garrett softly said, "John, my friend, please calm down, and I'll explain everything as I remember and what's been told to me."

"Right there, what does that mean?"

Garrett cocked his head; an annoyed look gripped his face. "John, stop talking, and I'll tell you everything."

John took a deep breath, exhaled and said, "Start from the beginning."

"How about I start from when you arrived in St. Joseph? That's the train memory I believe you're having."

"Yes, do that."

"One second, before I start, let me say you're one lucky son of a bitch."

"I heard that earlier," John said.

"Anyway, let's go back a month ago. I think that's a good place to start."

Garrett spent the greater part of three hours detailing the past month to John, who sat mostly quiet, only asking a few questions.

After Garrett finished, John looked away.

Seeing the pain on his face, Garrett said, "It's been a rough couple of weeks since. Like I said, we thought you weren't going to make it."

John didn't reply. He watched as the clouds slowly coursed across the blue sky.

"Can I get you something?" Garrett asked.

"So you two saved me?" John asked.

"She cradled you in her arms the entire time," Garrett said.

"Is she safe?" John asked.

"Yeah, she's fine."

"You say that with such confidence. How do you know she's fine?" John asked.

"Because she's here in Chicago," Garrett answered.

"She's here in Chicago?" John asked, his eyes wide with joy.

"She and Gabriel are staying at the York Hotel down the street from the hospital," Garrett replied.

"You've just told me the best news I've ever heard!" John exclaimed, his face beaming.

"She's been in here every day. She and Gabriel come and read to you. That woman is something else."

"I'd hug you if it wasn't so painful to do so," John said gleefully.

"However, there is something we do need to talk about."

"Now you're making me nervous," John said.

"It's a good thing, trust me. Technically we're all dead now, meaning we never made it out of St. Joseph alive. The head honcho here has given you, Helen and Gabriel new identities. You're new people now and can all make a new start on life. This was a request of Helen's. She wants to move past her life in Missouri and her connection to the James brothers. With her *dead*, no one should ever come looking again."

John nodded, his face stoic as he took in the seriousness of the revelation. A half grin suddenly appeared, as it was ironic that now Helen was living under an assumed name.

"You know something, she's supposed to be arriving soon," Garrett said, pulling out his pocket watch and checking the time.

As if on cue, the double doors swung open, and in came Helen and Gabriel.

Disregarding the pain, John sat up and cried out, "Helen!"

Hearing his voice, she, with Gabriel in tow, rushed to John's bedside.

Showing no concern for his injuries, John pulled her close and embraced her. "Oh, Helen, I feared the worst. I woke and I didn't know where I was, I couldn't remember; then Garrett told me everything. It all makes sense; how could he know those details without you telling him? Oh, Helen, I'm the happiest man," John said, tears freely flowing down his face.

"You've had me so worried," she said, holding him tight.

John looked up and saw Gabriel standing just behind her. "Hi, Gabriel."

"Hi, glad you're awake," Gabriel said.

"Me too, me too," John replied to Gabriel, his arms still wrapped around Helen.

"Have the doctors said when you can leave?" Helen asked, pulling away from him to get a better look.

"Not sure, I haven't spoken with them," John answered. "But I don't care, I'm leaving with you today."

"Are you sure you can?" Helen asked.

"No one is stopping me," John said.

Feeling like he was intruding on an intimate moment, Garrett picked up his hat and said to Gabriel, "How about you and I go down to the candy store on Clark Street? Word is they have the best caramels."

Gabriel's eyes widened with excitement. "Can I?" he asked Helen.

"Of course," she said with a smile. "Thank you, Garrett."

"Sure thing. And, Helen, his memory isn't so good; you might need to remind him of a few things," Garrett replied. The two walked off, with Gabriel chatting away like normal.

When they exited the ward, Helen took John's hand and brought it to her lips and kissed it. "I'm so happy to see you awake. We feared the worst."

"I keep hearing that," John said.

"'Cause it's true," she said.

"Well, doctors don't know what they're talking about," John said.

"You're lucky," she said.

"Another thing I keep hearing," he said.

"No, you are lucky. It's a miracle you fell from the house and down alongside some of the stone foundation. It protected you from the full force of the blast. And another thing, without the Pinkerton Detective Agency bringing you here, you might have died. This hospital has the best care outside of New York City."

"I suppose it does pay to know people," John quipped.

"I forgot to ask Garrett, but Sheriff Hooper, what was the word about him in St. Joseph afterwards?" John asked.

"They found pieces of him at the house and determined accurately he'd been murdered by the James brothers. As far as them, rumors are they actually did go to Nashville, although some have said they made their way to Texas."

"And the train?" John asked.

"Went on its way without incident," Helen answered.

"Enough of all that, I want to talk about our future," he said, squeezing her hand tenderly.

"California."

"Yes, there."

"We can go anywhere as long as we're together," she said.

"Tell me why we're going there," John said with hopes she'd jog his memory.

She gave him an odd look then recalled what Garrett had told her just before leaving. "You had read about some sort of oil that comes naturally from the ground. You told me you think it could be the next boom; in fact, you called it black gold."

"Yes, that's right. I read an article when I was traveling to St. Joseph. They quoted a professor from Yale. He was talking about all the commercial uses for it. Apparently it seeps out of the ground in the hills north of Los Angeles."

"Ojai, that's the name of the town you want to explore and prospect for this black gold," she said.

"Oil, black gold…hmm, you never know, it could be the next big thing, and I want us to be there to capitalize on it."

"Then we shall go there and prospect," she said.

He laughed.

"What's so funny?" she asked.

"I don't think they call it prospecting," he replied.

"Don't you prospect for gold?" she asked.

"Yes."

"And didn't you call it black gold?" she quipped.

"Fair enough," he said, pulling her close and kissing her on the lips. "You can call it whatever you want." He glanced at her left hand and saw a wedding band. He pulled back, pointed at the ring and exclaimed, "What's this?"

She held her hand up and blinked her eyes flirtatiously. "While you were unconscious, we got married."

"We did?" he asked.

"Not officially, but it's part of our new identities. I hope you don't mind, but I chose Davis as our last name."

"Davis?"

"Yes, it's an easy name to remember. We're now the Davis family, John, Helen and Gabriel Davis."

He shook his head and chuckled. "That's perfect." Once more he pulled her close and kissed her lips. He looked deeply into her blue eyes and said, "I love you."

"I love you, too," she replied sweetly.

"So California it will be. I hear it's beautiful out there. It'll be a good place to put roots down and start new."

"Yes," she said.

"I'll take you and Gabriel to the ocean, the great Pacific Ocean. I hear it's the biggest in the world," he said.

"That's sounds exciting and scary. I've never seen an ocean before. Does it look like that?" she asked, pointing out the window towards Lake Michigan, which sat across the street from the hospital.

He glanced out and replied, "I suppose it does. I've never been to the ocean either, only seen drawings in books."

The two held each other lovingly and stared out at the dark blue lake.

John's mind raced back to his days wandering the vast expanses of the United States…alone. He'd been to so many places and seen so many things but hadn't had anyone to share his journeys with. Now he was embarking on a new journey, one where he'd be able to share the joys and hardships with the woman he loved. He smiled as he thought that God was truly merciful.

Here he was, a deeply flawed man, yet God had given him a new chance at happiness, a chance he wouldn't squander. Never again would he allow allegiances to lost causes separate him from family. His only allegiance now was to Helen and Gabriel, and it was one he'd never tear apart.

## THE END

## READ AN EXCERPT FROM

## G. MICHAEL HOPF and A. AMAERICAN'S POST-APOCALYPTIC NOVEL

## HOPE

---

## CHAPTER ONE

"Hope is the word which God has written on the brow of every man." – Victor Hugo

### Descanso, CA

Charlotte wasn't sure if it was the throaty rumble of the truck engine pulling into their driveway or her father's voice ordering her and her little sister to go hide that she heard first. Not questioning him, she took Hope firmly by the hand and raced upstairs.

"What's happening, Charlotte?" her sister asked, her voice trembling.

"Somebody's coming and Daddy wants us to hide, like before," Charlotte replied, walking hand in hand into the master bedroom's walk-in closet. "Now just wait here; I'll be right back."

"No," Hope pleaded.

"I'm just going to get my diary, I need it."

Hope gripped Charlotte's hand tighter. Her eyes

widened as she again begged for Charlotte to stay. "I'm scared. Don't go."

"Hope, I'm just running into my room. I'll be right back."

"No," Hope replied as her little fingers squeezed hard.

"Hope, you're six; you're a big girl now. I'll just be a sec," Charlotte said and pulled away. She closed the closet door and ran to her bedroom just down the hall.

Charlotte could hear voices outside her window. Curious, she peered out to see an old pickup truck, and circling it were five men. Her father, not a small man, towered over them all. He was engaged in a heated conversation with a man she recognized seeing once before.

"I told you I don't know where it is," Charlotte's father hollered.

"Yeah, you do. You're the only one who would," the man replied.

"I told you already, I don't know, plus why would I ever cross you?"

"It's very easy, just tell me where it is and I'll let you and your little family live."

Charlotte watched the man spit out a large wad of tobacco juice. He grinned and said, "I'll give you one more chance, and if you don't tell us, I'll go in there, rip out your two pretty little girls, and have my boys here do unimaginable things to them."

"I told you I didn't take it."

Charlotte's heart pumped heavily and her hand

trembled with fear.

A commotion broke out as Charlotte's father produced a gun and waved it in front of the man. "Go away now, or I'll shoot you!"

Calmly the man stepped to the side and pulled out his own pistol and immediately shot Charlotte's father in the chest.

Charlotte gasped and stumbled backwards at the sight of her father falling to the ground. She tripped over the edge of the bed and hit the floor hard.

The creak of the front door hit her ears.

The man hollered, "Tear the place apart, boys. I want what is mine!"

Charlotte scrambled to her feet and sprinted from her bedroom towards the master bedroom, with her pink diary in her hand.

Back in the closet, she found Hope whimpering behind a row of clothes.

She closed the door and tucked up next to her.

A small box lay next to her; inside was a flashlight. She took it out and turned it on.

The bright light lit the dark space.

With a crackling voice, Hope asked, "What was that sound?"

Charlotte didn't reply; she opened her diary and began to write.

> *January 21*
> *Dear Mommy,*
> *The bad men came back. Daddy said they wouldn't and they did. Me and Hope are hiding in your closet.*

"Charlotte, where's Daddy?"

"Ssh, not so loud," Charlotte ordered.

"I want Dada." Hope began to sob. "I'm scared."

Charlotte looked up to see tears streaming down Hope's plump rosy cheeks. Knowing she had to comfort her but still determined to jot down what she could, she set the flashlight down in her lap and put her arm around Hope.

Hope melted into Charlotte's chest and cried.

*Mommy, I miss you. Where are you? How come you never came home? Daddy says it's because you were far away when the power went out. Are you mad at me? Did I do something to make you mad?*

Voices boomed from what sounded like the hallway.

Hope quivered.

Charlotte looked up at the door. She feared that at any moment it would open and they'd die like her father.

Looking back down at the eggshell-white paper, she began to write again.

*If I made you mad, I'm sorry. Please come home, we need you.*

The voices grew louder.

Hope's tears continued to flow and her body shook with fear.

Charlotte paused her writing. She asked if there was more to write. Had she written enough? Her father had told her to begin the diary soon after everything stopped working so she could have a connection with her mother and as a way for her to express the emotions she was feeling. She had taken to it almost instantly and found solace in the words she wrote daily. Charlotte looked at it as a form of communication, a series of letters and notes to her mother, who had never returned from a trip back to the Midwest she had taken a day before the world came to a grinding halt.

"Where's Dada? I want Dada," Hope moaned.

Not wanting to tell Hope what she saw, she lied, "I don't know where Dada is." This lie to her sister prompted her to reveal the truth to her mother.

*Daddy died today. The bad men killed him. They shot him out in front of the house for no reason. Hope is crying. She's scared.*

*Oh no, the bad men are now in your room. I'm scared. I think we're going to die. I don't want to die, Mommy, I don't want to die.*

The sound of heavy footfalls stopped just outside the closet door.

Charlotte questioned whether she had locked the door. To be sure, she reached up to verify and found the door unlocked. Her gut clenched and sweat formed on her brow. Delicately she pushed the pin that locked the handle and just in time.

The knob jiggled.

Charlotte slid back further into the closet until her back was against the wall.

Hope clung to her waist and whimpered.

Softly, Charlotte said, "Ssh."

The knob jiggled harder and the pressure of someone outside the door weighed against it.

Remembering the small revolver her father had left in the box just for this type of emergency, Charlotte reached in and grabbed it. The steel felt cold against the hot skin of her palm and the weight was heavy. She wrapped both her small hands around the grip and pointed it at the door.

"Hey, the door is locked!" a man barked from the other side of the door.

Hope and Charlotte drew closer, if that was even possible.

Charlotte's hand shook, making the loose cylinder of the revolver rattle.

"Kick it open!" another man's voice boomed. This was the voice of the man who'd shot Charlotte's father.

Charlotte tensed her body, waiting for the door to come crashing in at any moment, but nothing happened.

Voices called from further in the house.

The shadow underneath the door disappeared, gone as fast as it had appeared.

Charlotte gulped hard. A steady sweat poured down her face.

Hollers now echoed from the opposite side of the house.

"Are the bad men gone?" Hope whispered.

"I don't know," Charlotte said, lowering the revolver, her arms aching.

"I'm scared."

"Me too."

"Where's Dada?" Hope asked, lifting her head from Charlotte's lap.

"I don't know," Charlotte said, again not able to tell Hope the truth.

"Is Dada dead?"

Charlotte opened her mouth to reply but froze.

"Charlotte, is Dada dead?"

"I don't know."

"I heard something, was it a gun?"

Heavy footfalls came again and stopped just outside the door. "Open it up the old-fashioned way!"

"Will do!" a man replied.

Charlotte shook, her arms outstretched with the revolver.

The door exploded open.

Both girls screamed in terror.

The man froze when he saw the muzzle of the revolver pointed at him. "Now, take it easy there, little one," he said, his hand held out and motioning for her to put it down.

Charlotte's eyes were as wide as saucers. She placed her index finger on the trigger and began to apply pressure.

"Put the gun down, okay, sweetheart. Don't do nothin' stupid."

A second man appeared and chuckled when he saw the two girls. He turned to the first man and said with a pat on his back, "The boss will be happy."

The first man held him back and warned, "Dude, she has a gun."

"I know, I ain't blind, but I don't think that pretty little thing will do anything to me," he said with a toothy grin.

Charlotte's arms began to shake vigorously from a

combination of fear and fatigue.

"I don't know, man, she has a look in her eye," the first man said, taking a step back and out of the aim of Charlotte.

"She's just a little girl," the second man said and took another step inside the closet.

"Leave us alone!" Charlotte screamed.

"What's your name?" the second man asked as he knelt down a few feet from her.

"Leave!"

"We won't hurt you, I promise."

Tears flowed down Charlotte's face. "Leave."

Hope was crying uncontrollably.

With his hand out in front of him, the man repeated, "We won't hurt you, I promise."

"You killed..."

"Your father didn't cooperate; he was a stupid man. Don't be like your daddy, girl."

"Dada!" Hope wailed.

"Leave or I'll shoot!" Charlotte barked.

"It would be irresponsible for us to leave you here alone. There's a lot of bad people out there."

"Leave!"

The man shifted quickly to the right, but with his left hand he snatched the revolver and twisted it out of Charlotte's hand.

Charlotte and Hope both curled up tight and recoiled as far as they could, their backs planted firmly against the cold wall.

The man stood, looked at the other man, and said,

"If we don't find the other shit, at least the day wasn't a total loss."

# CHAPTER TWO

"Hope is the pillar that holds up the world. Hope is the dream of a waking man." – Pliny the Elder

## El Centro, CA

Neal opened his eyes and stared towards the popcorn-white ceiling. His insomnia was becoming unbearable, but what were his choices? He thought about taking the sleeping pills he had found, but the thought of drugging himself just felt wrong.

The full moon cast its light through his bedroom window and provided him a reprieve from the intense darkness that he was accustomed to living with during these late hours. Taking advantage of a bad situation, he pressed his eyes closed and ran through the plan for the day in his mind. He was someone who believed in creative visualization and had done it often during his college football days. Now instead of visualizing successful catches, he'd process each step he would make, each turn and every doorway he'd shadow, with the outcome being positive with his safe return.

Finished with his exercise, he glanced towards the darkened digital alarm clock. It was a habit he hadn't been able to kick even though the red glowing lights hadn't shown for eight months. His guess was it was sometime after three in the morning, his normal wake-up time these days.

Putting his attention back on the ceiling, he began to recite the things he was grateful for. Like his visual exercise, this had become another ritual and one that kept him a bit sane and thinking positive. His wife, Karen, was always the first on the list he'd think of, not because she was lying next to him sleeping but because he wouldn't have been able to keep it together much less survive the past months without her. Second was his eight-year-old daughter, Beth. She was the twinkle in his eye, the light of his life, and many people often referred to her as his twin. There was no mistaking her as his daughter. Karen would often joke that the only reason she knew Beth was hers was because she gave birth to her. Third on his list was Carlos, his neighbor and friend for many years. Together, they had managed to secure food, water and additional supplies. Carlos was a mechanic by trade and fortunately for them also collected old classic hot rods, which came in handy since many modern vehicles had ceased to work.

While he went through his list, many faces of those he had known would come to mind, other neighbors, co-workers and even the familiar faces he'd see on a regular basis at the store or coffee shop. All gone or not seen since the blackout. All of his and Carlos' neighbors had packed up and left, many on foot. Their final destination was the rumored FEMA camp in Yuma, Arizona. If there was anything that remained a sure thing, it was the rumor mill. Within hours of the blackout, rumors flew. Many gathered that a terrorist attack had occurred, and practically thinking, it made sense. Soon the rumors came that the federal government was mobilizing a response to the crisis and establishing relief camps in Riverside. This rumor was proven fact when a small convoy from the Department of Homeland Security passed through, plastering leaflets. Not long afterwards came the US Postal Service. They moved through town, taking a survey of the residents and giving them instructions. Like a levee breaking, the residents of El Centro, a small desert city one hundred and eighteen miles east of San Diego, flooded out, all headed for Yuma and the promise of salvation.

Neal and Carlos resisted the call to leave. Neal and Carlos avoided the mailmen and their DHS security teams. With everyone gone, they factored their ability to sustain themselves was greater with a majority of the population gone. Their theory proved correct. With most people gone, they found an abundance of food, water and supplies. As the days turned to weeks then into months, they had become so accustomed to their new lives that the world of before seemed like a dream. The abandoned cars that littered the highway and streets became a nuisance not a reminder. When the water stopped flowing, the acres upon acres of crops that surrounded the city had surrendered the green crops to the desert. The massive transmission towers were silent; the crackling of electricity that used to flow through them shut off that day and never came back on. They now stood as relics of an age that neither man believed was coming back. Everything around them represented a time of ease, abundance and in many ways decadence.

Neal began his daily ritual of gratitude because he wanted to remain positive but also because he knew the day of coasting would come to an end. They had managed to survive without the problems many had suffered. Not a week would go by without them encountering a wandering pack of people. For the most part they kept their distance, but occasionally they had conversations. The news from around the country wasn't good. The blackout had affected the entire nation from coast to coast. Everything was down; the entire electrical grid had collapsed along with most devices that had solid-state components. With the grid, society itself fell. The federal government's response hadn't been what the people expected, with rumors of people being gathered and systematically removed or, as some wanderers put it, people had just disappeared.

Carlos and Neal listened to the stories and didn't know what to believe. All they knew was their decision to stay had worked, but the day would come when something really bad would happen. This thought would nag Neal daily. Like a hovering mosquito that wouldn't go away regardless of how many times you batted the air, the dark images of his family suffering would plague his mind. He had no issues with something happening to him, he even could tolerate Karen getting hurt, but any image of Beth in trouble made him nauseous. It was a parent's responsibility to protect their children and die before them. If there was one thing that haunted him, it was that, losing Beth.

"I can hear you thinking," Karen mumbled under her breath.

"You're awake?"

Karen rolled onto her back and snuggled up to Neal. "Yeah, been awake for a while."

"You good?" Neal asked.

"It's never going to be the same, is it?"

"Nope."

"It's just so weird. You know, I don't miss the old world."

Neal turned his head and asked, "Really? I don't believe that for one second. You loved your reality shows, and I swear you went through withdrawals without your Starbucks macchiatos."

"Reality TV, no, but yes, I do miss my Starbucks."

"I miss ice cream. I can see it now; hell, I can taste it when I think about chocolate peanut butter Haagen-Dazs."

"And that, I miss that too," Karen mused and drew closer.

"Does it sound odd to say I miss McDonald's French fries?" Neal joked.

"McDonald's? When did you eat McDonald's?"

"Well…"

"Secrets? Now I hear about dark secrets?"

"I wouldn't call grabbing a large fry now and then a dark secret."

"What else have you kept from me?" Karen prodded.

"Besides all my mistresses, nothing," he joked.

She jabbed him in the side with her elbow. "You better be kidding."

"Ouch, I am, geez."

"Anything else?"

"No, no other secrets."

"Not that, anything you really miss."

"A good sci-fi movie."

"I miss pizza. Don't ask me why, but a nice thin crust with roasted garlic, sausage, onion and mushroom sounds good right about now."

"Pizza at three a.m.?"

"Anytime, God, my mouth is watering thinking about it."

Neal leaned close and gave her a full kiss on the mouth.

She returned his kiss and began to caress his body. She stopped, pulled away slightly, and said, "I don't miss the spare tire you were carrying. You look and feel good," she purred.

"If only I knew the apocalypse diet was the one way to bring back my lean and mean twenty something look, I would've done it long ago."

She ran her hand across his chest and belly. "Wow."

He leaned in and kissed her again, this time more firmly and passionately.

"I'm scared," whispered Beth from the doorway.

Neal and Karen jumped.

"What is it, sweetheart?" Karen asked.

Beth pushed the cracked door fully open and entered the moonlit room. "I had a bad dream."

Karen got out of bed, approached Beth, and gave her a warm embrace. "Come on, honey, let's get you back in bed."

Beth stood firm and asked, "Can I sleep with you and Daddy?"

Karen looked towards Neal, who sat up and shrugged his shoulders.

"No, honey, you should sleep in your own bed," Karen replied. Normally Karen would have said yes, but tonight she hoped to return and continue the intimate moment she and Neal had been having.

"No, Mommy, I'm really scared," Beth resisted.

"Come, Beth, let's go back to bed. It was just a bad dream."

"I dreamed you died," Beth cried out with tears following.

Karen knelt and gave her another embrace. "It's okay, sweetie. It was just a bad dream, nothing more."

"I saw you, you were there, dead," Beth said, pointing towards the bed.

Karen petted her hair and attempted to comfort her.

"Your eyes were open, but they just stared. You were dead, Mommy, you were dead," Beth cried.

"Karen, it's okay. She can jump in bed with us," Neal said softly.

"Come on, baby, jump in bed with us," Karen said, taking her by the hand and escorting her to the bed.

Beth and Karen both got in the bed with Beth snuggled between them.

Neal leaned over and gave Beth a dozen small kisses on her cheeks and forehead. "So, Mommy and I were talking about what we've missed since the power stopped. So far on the list we have ice cream, sci-fi movies, French fries, pizza…"

Excited to take part in the conversation, Beth blurted out, "Mac and cheese."

"Yeah, mac and cheese, I miss that too," Neal said.

"But not with any of that yucky stuff you put on it," Beth countered.

"What yucky stuff?" Neal asked.

"The hot sauce," Beth replied.

"You just need to acquire the taste, that's all," Neal said, defending his use of Tapatio hot sauce.

Karen tickled Beth and said, "I agree with you, yucky."

"Whatever, all I know is hot sauce is proof that God loves us."

Karen rolled her eyes even though Neal couldn't see. It wasn't a gesture out of contempt but one of love. She and Neal had met nine years before and one thing that she loved about his personality was his humor. He was the one man that made her truly laugh.

"I miss my friends," Beth said.

"You do?" Neal asked.

"Yeah, I miss Ella the most."

"I know, you two were besties," Karen said, rubbing Beth's arm.

"Are they still alive?" Beth asked.

The question threw Karen and Neal. "Why would you ask that?" Neal asked.

"I heard you and Mom talking about seeing people dead and…"

Karen leaned in and asked, "And what?"

"I heard Daddy say something about wondering if the Reynolds and your other friends were dead."

Karen sighed. "We were just talking."

Neal sat up, cleared his throat, and replied bluntly, "Honey, the world has changed and not exactly for the best. It's different and, well…"

"What were you about to say?" Karen asked him.

"It's time we were honest with her."

"No, she's just a little girl."

"Karen, she needs to know, not the gruesome details, but we can't shield her from the realities out there."

"No," Karen insisted.

"Karen, I'm just going to chat with her. She's going to find out one way or another and I'd rather have her hear it from me directly than to overhear me and not understand the context."

Karen thought for a second before replying, "How about we discuss what you're thinking of saying?"

Neal also paused before responding. "Fine."

"Tell me," Beth urged.

"No, your mother's right. We both will discuss what's happening out there, but do it later."

"C'mon."

"No, now get some sleep," Karen said.

Beth crossed her arms and grunted.

Neal leaned in and kissed her on the forehead. "Get some sleep."

Beth grumbled.

He got closer and whispered into her ear, "And I don't think Ella and her parents are dead. I was just wondering. After a lot of thought I came to the conclusion they were fine. Ella's daddy is a smart guy; I'm sure he got to Ella's grandparents' house safe and sound."

"You sure?"

"Yes, now close your eyes. I need you bright eyed and bushy tailed in the morning, you've gotta help Mommy inventory the pantry."

"Okay, love you, Dada."

"Love you too."

"Love you, Mama."

Karen kissed her and whispered, "Love you, baby."

Neal rolled onto his back and immediately thoughts of the Reynolds came rushing in. He didn't know for sure if they were safe, but telling Beth they were did ease her mind. Was that right for him to do? Being a parent was not an easy job, and those who thought it was were usually not parents. When you first discovered you'd be a parent, you really didn't know what to expect. Yes, many people experienced joy but also fear came. Would you be a good parent? Would you have all the answers? Would your kids grow up to be good people? There had been many books written on parenting, but were any of them correct? How did you talk to a child about the apocalypse? he asked himself. Just how did you begin that conversation, over a family dinner? 'Hi, Beth, the world as you know it just ended and you may not survive. Do you want rice or beans?' He had thought before of discussing what happened with her, but he never could find that right moment. Now with her asking questions like she just did, he knew it was the time.

It didn't take long for Beth to fall back to sleep. Her heavy and rhythmic breathing gave him peace, but it was now time for him to get up and prepare for the long day ahead.

CONTINUE READING ON AMAZON

## ABOUT THE AUTHOR

G. Michael Hopf is the best-selling author of THE NEW WORLD series and other apocalyptic novels. He spent two decades living a life of adventure before he settled down and became a novelist full time. He is a combat veteran of the Marine Corps and a former executive protection agent. He lives with his family in San Diego, CA

Please feel free to contact him at geoff@gmichaelhopf.com with any questions or comments.

www.gmichaelhopf.com

www.facebook.com/gmichaelhopf

TORN ALLEGIANCE

BOOKS by G. MICHAEL HOPF

## THE NEW WORLD SERIES

THE END
THE LONG ROAD
SANCTUARY
THE LINE OF DEPARTURE
BLOOD, SWEAT & TEARS
THE RAZOR'S EDGE
THOSE WHO REMAIN

## NEW WORLD SERIES SPIN OFFS

NEMESIS: INCEPTION
EXIT

## THE WANDERER SERIES

VENGEANCE ROAD
BLOOD GOLD
TORN ALLEGIANCE

## ADDITIONAL BOOKS

HOPE (CO-AUTHORED W/ A. AMERICAN)
DAY OF RECKONING
MOTHER (EXTINCTION CYCLE SERIES)
DETACHMENT (PERSEID COLLAPSE SERIES)
DRIVER 8: A POST-APOCALYPTIC NOVEL

G. MICHAEL HOPF